Edward Sabine Renwick

The Thermostatic Incubator

Its construction and management, together with descriptions of brooders,

nurseries

Edward Sabine Renwick

The Thermostatic Incubator
Its construction and management, together with descriptions of brooders, nurseries

ISBN/EAN: 9783337381950

Printed in Europe, USA, Canada, Australia, Japan

Cover: Foto ©Andreas Hilbeck / pixelio.de

More available books at **www.hansebooks.com**

THE

Thermostatic Incubator,

ITS CONSTRUCTION AND MANAGEMENT,

TOGETHER WITH DESCRIPTIONS OF

BROODERS, NURSERIES,

And the Mode of Raising Chickens by Hand.

BY

E. S. RENWICK,

MECHANICAL ENGINEER AND EXPERT.

PUBLISHED BY THE AUTHOR.

NEW YORK:

BURR PRINTING HOUSE.

1883.

CONTENTS.

INTRODUCTION.

THE Thermostatic Incubator furnishes an efficient and reliable means of hatching chickens artificially. It is the result of numerous experiments, and as its principal features have been thoroughly tested for seven seasons, and it has been successfully used in its present form for two, it is confidently offered for public use. It is adapted to hatch ducks' eggs, as well as those of chickens, the author having hatched with it an average of 250 chickens and 40 ducks annually ; which is as large a number as his family can dispose of. Partridge eggs have also been hatched in it, with perfect success.

As the experience of the author may be of service to others working in the same field, and a statement of it will enable the construction of the apparatus to be better understood, it may be worth while to give a sketch of his labors. The subject was taken up in 1873 as an amusement, and as a means of divert-

ing the mind from the cares of an arduous profes-
sional business. The raising of fancy chickens had
been a hobby for years, and the various published
statements of the methods of hatching chickens artificially had been carefully studied. As the resi-
dence of the author was heated by steam, it was
thought that a sufficiently equable heat could be
obtained from the top of the steam boiler to do the
work of incubation. Hence an incubator was constructed with two drawers, one above the other, and
with the lower edges of its sides curved to fit the
top of the brick casing of the steam boiler ; a thermometer was placed in this incubator, and it was
found that there was sufficient heat for the purpose.
The accounts of the various incubators made by
others had informed the author that there were
three things essential to successful artificial incubation ; viz., an equable temperature, ventilation, and
moisture. Moisture had been supplied by Bonne-
main and his successors, by placing pans of water
in the incubator beneath the eggs. Ventilation had
also been effected by admitting air to the lower part
of the incubator, and allowing the hot or foul air to
escape from its top. Following in the steps of his
predecessors in the art, the author fitted his first incubator with a water trough beneath the egg drawers, and with holes for the admission of fresh air,
which was distributed beneath the egg drawers by
means of metal plates. A ventilating hole also was
made at the top, and was fitted with a damper
valve, which was to be opened and closed for the
purpose of varying the draught of air through the incubator and thus regulating the heat. The damper

valve was operated by a very large alcoholic thermometer, holding half a pint of alcohol, which was
closed to the air by an inverted syphon pipe containing mercury on which a float was placed ; and
the float was connected with the ventilating valve.
This alcoholic thermometer proved too sluggish for
any practical use, and was abandoned after a trial of
three days. A second attempt was made to operate
the ventilating valve, and thereby regulate the heat,
by means of a large mercurial thermometer, the
bulb of which was of iron and contained a pound of
mercury. This also proved to be too sluggish, as it
required a variation of 20° Fahrenheit in the egg
chamber to make it operate the valve sufficiently.
A third attempt was made with a thermostat constructed of brass rods and glass tubes arranged like
the bars of a compensation gridiron pendulum ; the
requisite amount of movement being obtained by a
system of multiplying levers. This also proved im-.
practicable as a means for opening the valve within
the required limits of temperature. The author
then came to the conclusion that it was expedient
to use a thermometer only to determine the temperature at which the valve was to be moved, and to
rely upon some other force to operate the regulating valve. He also determined to move the incubator into his work-room and to use lamps to
furnish the heat, as this course would enable him to
continue his experiments while the steam boiler for
heating the house was not in use.

Upon determining to use lamps, the first problem
that presented itself was the regulation of the heat
supplied by them. Ordinary kerosene lamps require

so much force to turn the wick up and down that it seemed useless to attempt to regulate the heat in that manner. The author knew of the use of sliding wick tubes for varying the flame of the spirit lamps used in chemical laboratories, but feared that these might become so clogged by crusts or deposits from the flame that their free movement would be prevented ; he therefore gave up the idea of using them, and finally came to the conclusion that the easiest way to regulate the heat would be to permit the flame of the lamp to burn regularly as it might be set by hand ; and to either use the heat, or to let it escape without materially heating the incubator, as the heat of the incubating chamber fell or rose. In order to operate upon this system, the author invented his waste heat chimney, which in its simplest form is a chimney arranged within the ordinary chimney or flue of a lamp, and fitted at its upper end with a valve. When this valve is closed, the hot products of combustion from the lamp are compelled to pass between the central waste heat chimney and the ordinary chimney or flue ; and the walls of the latter being thereby heated transmit heat to the incubator. When, on the other hand, the damper valve is opened, the products of combustion take the direct course through the waste heat chimney and escape at its upper end, leaving the outer flue unheated. The operation of this contrivance is attended with an incidental operation which was not anticipated, but which is important. When the heat passes through the waste heat chimney, the draught is much stronger than when the heat is passing through the

outer flue ; and the effect of this stronger draught is
to cause the air which enters the cone or deflector of
the lamp to be deflected more forcibly against the
flame at the flame slot of the burner, and consequently to reduce the volume of the flame. Hence
the opening of the valve or damper of the waste
heat chimney not only allows the heat to waste, but
also causes a reduction of the flame, so that the heat
given out by the lamp is reduced ; while the closing
of the valve of the waste heat chimney not only
utilizes the heat, but also causes the flame to increase in volume. The two movements of the
valve therefore produce incidentally effects upon the
flame similar to those of lowering and raising the
lamp wick.

The next matter to be decided was the means of
circulating the heat through the incubator, and for
this purpose water heaters were used operating upon
the plan employed to heat green-houses. Two
lamps were employed for heating, and a separate
water heater was employed for each lamp. Each
heater consisted of an endless pipe of rectangular
cross-section, constructed in the form of a square
ring and set on edge. A pipe or flue was soldered
into one of the sides of this ring heater, so that the
heated gases from the lamp might pass through this
flue, and heat the water surrounding it. The water
so heated rose in the upright side of the pipe heater,
circulated horizontally along the upper horizontal
part of the heater, descended through the opposite
upright side, and passed horizontally along the lower
horizontal part back to the first upright side of the
heater in which the flue was situated, thus making a

continuous circulation. The two water heaters were
placed edge to edge but were reversed right and left,
the lamps being at opposite ends of the incubator,
so that the current in one heater circulated along
the upper part of the incubator from right to left,
and the current in the other circulated in the opposite direction, thus equalizing the heat in the incubating chamber.

The two drawers for eggs were arranged one over
the other, and slid on rails through the rectangular
space within the ring pipes. A waste heat chimney
was secured in each lamp flue ; and a damper valve
capable of being turned edgewise or flatwise, was arranged in the upper end of each of these chimneys
so that the heat from the lamp might either be permitted to waste through the chimney, or be compelled to heat the flue and the water of the heater
surrounding it.

For the purpose of moving the damper valves,
the author determined to use springs controlled by
electro-magnets, the circuit of electricity for which
should be made and broken by the action of a thermometer. The first thermometer which the author
planned for the purpose was one like Six's registering thermometer, with a large upright bulb containing methyline, which moved a column of mercury.
A platinum wire was soldered into the lower bend
of the syphon tube so as to make a constant com-
munication between the galvanic battery and the
mercury. A second platinum wire was soldered in
a downward direction into the descending branch of
the tube in which the methylene expanded, the end
of the wire being set at the point at which the mer-

cury would be when the temperature was 98° Fahrenheit. A third platinum wire was introduced into the open ascending branch of the syphon pipe, with its lower end at the point at which the mercury would be at 105° Fahrenheit. The operation expected was that while the temperature should be between 98° and 105°, the mercury would not make electric contact with either the second or third wires, but that both of them would be surrounded by the methylene, which is a non-conductor of electricity. Consequently so long as this condition of things lasted, no electricity would be conducted from the battery, and the valves would remain at rest. When, however, the temperature should sink to 98° Fahrenheit, the mercury would make an electric connection between the first and second wires ; and when on the other hand the temperature rose to 105° Fahrenheit, the mercury would make an electrical connection between the first and third wires. Two electro-magnets were used, and also two valve engines worked by springs ; the one to open the valves, and the other to close them. Each valve engine consisted of a train of wheels like a clock movement with a clock spring to furnish the motive power, and a fly to regulate the speed ; and each operated a reciprocating pawl which moved a ratchet wheel secured to the valve shaft ; one valve engine turning the valve shaft to the right hand, to open the valves ; and the other valve engine turning the valve shaft to the left to close the valves. Each valve engine was provided with a detent operated by its appropriate electro-magnet, so that when the circuit to that magnet was made by the upward movement of the mercury in the corresponding arm of the thermometer syphon, the detent was operated, and the valve engine was permitted to work and to move the valves.

An electric switch was introduced into each circuit, and a connection made between the valve shaft and these two switches so that whenever one of the valve engines had worked sufficiently (to open or close the valve) the switch appertaining to the electro-magnet of that engine was opened and the electric current was broken notwithstanding the continuance of the connection made by the mercury of the thermometer. The other switch was simultaneously shut so as to make the electric circuit for the other valve engine complete except the gap to be filled by the movement of the mercury of the thermometer ; consequently whenever the mercury was moved sufficiently by the variation of temperature, the electric circuit for the valve engine was completed. The thermometer was arranged upright at the rear of the egg drawers, and the foul air was permitted to escape at the top of the incubator through a short pipe ; the escape being regulated by a damper valve that was opened and closed with the waste heat valves, so that whenever the heat within the incubator rose to 105° the draught of air through it was increased simultaneously with the shutting off of heat from the lamps.

When this apparatus was set at work with several thermometers distributed in the drawers, certain defects were speedily demonstrated. In the first place it was found that the upper drawer had an average of eight degrees higher temperature than the lower, although the difference in level did not exceed four inches. In the second place, it was found that the fresh air admitted at the bottom of the incubator did not distribute itself equably throughout it, but formed currents, taking about the shortest lines from the entry orifices to the escape orifice at the top, while eddies were apparently formed in other parts. Hence the temperature at different parts of the same drawer, and at the same level in the incubator, varied materially ; and although the difficulty was overcome to some extent by introducing perforated diaphragms beneath the drawers to distribute the air, this plan proved unsatisfactory. Another defect was the vertical arrangement of the thermometer bulb, which caused its upper end to be materially hotter than its lower end. Another difficulty arose from the fact that the methylene of the thermometer prevented an immediate electric connection between the mercury and the platinum wire ; hence the mercury would sometimes rise half an inch above the end of the wire in the methylene of the thermometer before the electric circuit would be completed.

These defects rendered it useless to attempt to hatch eggs with the incubator, and it was determined to reconstruct it, using the same egg drawers. To obviate the first defect, the two egg drawers were placed side by side at the same level. To obviate the second defect, a new system of ventilating an incubator was devised which has proved to be one of the essentials of success for artificial incubation, and for which, among other improvements, the author has received a patent (No. 193,616, A.D. 1877).

According to this system, the fresh air for ventilation is admitted into the incubating chamber *at its top*, while the air in the chamber is drawn off *nearer its bottom*. The warm air is thus forced to circulate *downward* against its natural upward tendency ; and the practical result is that local currents do not form, and the air arranges itself in layers or strata which sink gradually and are of nearly uniform temperature at the same level throughout the incubating chamber.

A new thermometer was procured with a horizontal methylene bulb connecting with an upright inverted syphon pipe for mercury ; and a steel float swimming upon the mercury was used to communicate motion to the switches for making the electric circuits for the electro-magnets. For this purpose the float was suspended from one arm of a balance lever which it moved. This lever also carried suspended from each arm an inverted **U** shaped platinum wire, having its ends arranged to dip into two mercury cups connected with the circuit wires. The connection between the float and the balance lever was so adjusted that when the temperature was midway between the two extreme limits, the balance lever was level, and neither wire was dipped into the mercury cups ; when, however, the float was lowered by a fall of temperature, the lever tipped and one of the bent wires or switches was lowered into one pair of the mercury cups and completed the circuit of one electro-magnet, while the second switch was raised ; and when the float rose, by the rise of the temperature, the second switch was lowered to complete the circuit of the second electro-magnet, while the first switch was raised. The clock mechanism for moving the valves, and the system of breaking the circuit by the movement of the valve shaft, after the valves had been moved the proper distance by either valve engine, were used as before.

In order that the regulating thermometer might be affected by the mean temperature of the two egg drawers, the thermometer was placed in the base of the ventilating chimney for the foul air. This base was formed by the space between the slides or rails of the adjacent sides of the two drawers, which thus became a chamber for the thermometer. The syphon pipe for the float protruded at the front of the incubator ; and the balance beam from which the float was suspended, was supported on a column in a glass case on top of the incubator.

The fresh air for ventilation was supplied through two air pipes at each end of the incubator. One of these pipes was a simple pipe rising in the incubating chamber from an aperture in the end near the bottom of the incubating chamber to within a short distance of its top. The other pipe was passed through the water heater ; it connected at its lower end with a hole in the bottom of the incubator, and its upper end delivered the air near the top of the incubator. By this arrangement, one of the pipes at each end could be used to supply air of the temperature of the atmosphere, while the other (which passed through the water heater) supplied air which was warmed by its passage through the water heater ; and either or both ventilating pipes could be used at pleasure.

In order that moisture might be supplied, water

pans were placed beneath the egg drawers, and sponges were placed in them to furnish an evaporating surface. As, however, the circulation of the air within the incubator was to be downward, additional evaporating pans were placed above the eggs so as to supply the hottest air with moisture, which would be carried down to the eggs by the descending circulation of air. One of these upper evaporating pans was suspended over each egg drawer, and was supplied with water from a water bottle placed on top of the incubator and delivering the water to the evaporator through a small pipe ; the supply being regulated by a stopcock. Each upper evaporator was provided with an overflow pipe, so that any surplus of water dropped into the pan under the eggs. This under pan also had an overflow pipe, delivering the surplus water into a vessel under the incubator.

The first trial of this new incubator with two thermometers in each drawer, demonstrated that it would operate satisfactorily. The heat throughout both egg drawers was practically uniform, the variation in horizontal directions being less than one degree ; while the temperature could be maintained by the regulating mechanism within one degree of Fahrenheit. It was fully tested for a month with thermometers in the drawers ; then, eight fresh eggs were put into the drawers, one in each corner of each drawer, and the machine was put regularly at work. About ten days after starting, some eggs that had been set upon by hens for a week were also put into the incubator. The first chicken was hatched from one of the fresh eggs on the nineteenth day, and the others came before the end of the twenty-first. After these first chickens were hatched, the drawers were progressively filled with fresh eggs, and 160 chickens and a number of ducklings were hatched that season. In fact the incubator, so far as the hatching of chickens from fresh eggs (without preliminary sitting under a hen) was concerned, was practically perfect, and experience demonstrated that it would hatch every fertile egg. Substantially the same incubator was used three seasons ; but, as the electro-magnetic mechanism was costly, and the thermometer and float mechanism were too delicate for common use, it was determined to get rid of them. Accordingly, after the first season's work was completed, a thermostat was made of strips of vulcanized India-rubber and of brass riveted together, and the change of form of the compound bars by heat was employed to operate the detent of the valve engine. The valves of the waste heat chimneys, and of the ventilating chimney, were arranged to revolve, so that a quarter of a revolution of the valve shaft would open the valves, and the next quarter of a revolution in the same direction would close them. But one valve engine was used to do all the work. A weight also was substituted for a spring in working the valve engine ; the weight being arranged as in the common Cuckoo clocks. A drawer for young chickens was placed on top of the incubator, and the warm air escaping through the ventilating chimney was permitted to pass through this drawer, the temperature of which was thus maintained at about 90° Fahrenheit.

It was deemed important that there should always

be a sufficient excess of force in the driving weight
of the valve engine to insure the movement of the
valves even in case of an accidental increase of friction ; but as such excess of weight would tend to
cause the valve engine to move with great speed,
and would cause the detent arms to strike the detent with a jar, a speed controller became necessary.
A fly controller, such as is used in the striking
movements of clocks, requires a train of cog gearing
to drive it at the requisite speed, and was therefore
deemed objectionable.   Hence a liquid speed controller was made by arranging a four-bladed paddle-
wheel to revolve in a trough of water nearly fitting
the paddles, and the paddle-wheel was mounted
upon and secured to the valve shaft, so that the
valve shaft could be turned by the weight no faster
than the water would permit the paddles to revolve.
This contrivance works almost without friction, and
controls the speed admirably, preventing any jar or
slam.

The water heaters, egg drawers, air supply pipes,
and evaporators remained unchanged.

Upon testing the incubator fitted with the thermostat it was found that the pressure of the detent
arms against the detent operated by the thermostat
was sufficient to hamper the movement of the latter.
To obviate this defect, the detent arms were removed from the main shaft of the valve engine, and
a separate shaft was added, and was connected with
the main shaft by cog-wheels, so as to make a complete revolution (in place of a quarter of a revolution) for each revolution of the main shaft.   This
modification reduced the pressure against the detent

to only one quarter of what it had been ; but it also required the reduction of the detent arms to a single one. To make this arm operate both for opening and closing the valves, two detents were placed side by side on the rock shaft with which the thermostat was connected ; the detent arm was constructed to vibrate crosswise of its plane of revolution ; the end of the detent arm was made in the form of a **T** ; and a self-acting switch was placed in its plane of revolution, so that the detent arm during each revolution was moved laterally by the switch, and was caused to operate alternately upon each detent. This contrivance worked well, and the incubator with it was kept in continuous operation, hatching chickens, for four months. The switch arrangement was not however as good a contrivance as the inventor deemed desirable ; hence while the incubator was in operation he devised a new plan of valve engine, in which two detents were used ; the first or regulator detent being operated by the thermostat, and controlling the action of a light spring, while the second detent was operated by this spring, and controlled the action of the weight of the valve engine. By this contrivance the resistance presented by the valve engine to the movement of the regulator detent by the thermostat, was reduced to the friction caused by the pressure of the light spring ; and the thermostat was relieved of the labor of operating the main or engine detent which controlled the action of the weight of the valve engine. As the light spring ran down partially at each operation, a connection was made between it and the main shaft of the valve engine, so that, whenever the latter turned to operate the valves, it wound up the light detent spring as much as the latter had run down in operating the second or engine detent. The connection between the spring and the main detent was made by means of two light cog-wheels. This new form of valve engine worked admirably, and it left nothing further to be desired in that direction. The incubator, however, still contained water heaters for circulating the heat, and the author determined to dispense with these, and to circulate the heat through the incubator by the air employed for ventilation. To accomplish this, the ascending air supply pipes were made large enough to receive within them the upright flues of the lamps ; the space between the exterior of the lamp flue and the interior of the air supply pipe being about half an inch broad all round the lamp flue. The heat, radiated into each of the two air supply pipes by the lamp flue within it, caused currents of air to set upward through them ; and this air, being heated in its upward passage, and escaping at the upper ends of the air supply pipes, distributed the heat through the incubating chamber. The lamp flue, after ascending through the air supply pipe nearly to the top of the incubating chamber, was conducted horizontally toward its centre, and was fitted with an escape pipe passing through the top of the incubator, so that a large radiating surface was provided in the top of the incubating chamber. In order to supply moisture to the large quantity of air which would pass through the incubating chamber, it was deemed inexpedient to rely upon spontaneous evaporation ; consequently an

evaporating pan was applied to the head of each upright lamp flue, and provision was made to supply
each evaporating pan constantly and automatically
with water from a font on top of the incubator.

Upon testing the apparatus with this hot air system
of heating, it was found that the heat could be
maintained within the required limits as easily as
with the water heaters ; but the quantity of water
required for moistening the air had been overesti-
mated, and the air became so thoroughly saturated
with moisture that as it cooled, while moving downward to the level of the base of the ventilating chimney, a portion of the water was deposited upon the
eggs and stopped the pores of the egg shells. Such
a stoppage, if complete, is fatal to incubation; because,
although the hatching of the germ under such circumstances commences and proceeds regularly for
some days, death takes place sooner or later by
suffocation. The excessive supply of moisture was
corrected by reducing the evaporators to half their
first dimensions, and then the incubator worked
admirably, hatching every fertile egg up to the time
of breaking the shell ; at which crisis (as is always
the case with eggs from parents too closely related)
a small percentage of chickens are sometimes unable
to free themselves by reason of some malformation,
or a wrong position of the beak ; it being occasionally the case that the head of a chicken in the egg is
tucked under one leg, or that the beak is deformed
so that it does not pierce the shell.

The success of the hot air system, with supplementary evaporation automatically regulated in
quantity, has been so well demonstrated by constant

use, that it is believed it must supersede the system of water heating ; particularly as it enables a large supply of fresh air to be circulated through the incubating chamber, without an excessive loss of heat. Consequently the author now employs this system exclusively. The descending system of ventilating the incubating chamber devised by the author, insures the heating of the upper sides of the eggs hotter than their lower sides, as is the case with eggs under a hen ; while the supply of moisture above the eggs insures the saturation of the hot air with moisture before it comes in contact with the eggs, so that they are not materially deprived of it. With the usual hot water system of distributing the heat, it is necessary to wet the eggs frequently by dipping them in warm water. The system now used by the author renders such dipping unnecessary ; while the automatic supply of water by means of fonts, operating upon the principle of the bird fountain, keeps the evaporation constant, and renders it easy to observe the quantity used.

As to the temperature required to hatch eggs successfully, the views gathered by the author from the information published on that subject at first led him to believe that only a minute variation from a certain temperature was permissible. This temperature was stated to be 104° or 105° Fahrenheit. In order to test the correctness of this temperature, the author applied a delicate recording thermometer to the breast of a sitting hen, and found the temperature to be 106°. It was, however, manifest that the egg during hatching cannot attain this temperature, because its upper side only is next to the hen, while its lower side is in contact with the ground. In order to ascertain the internal temperature of the egg, the end of one was pierced with a hole of sufficient size to admit a thermometer bulb ; a little carbolic acid was mixed with the contents to prevent putrification ; the thermometer bulb was inserted centrally, and the crevice around the thermometer tube was closed with plaster of Paris. The egg thus prepared was placed under a sitting hen, and in the centre of a clutch of eggs that had been set upon for several days. The temperature of the egg at the time was 65°. The temperature rose to 98°, and then remained constant during the day. Early the next morning, the temperature was 96°. It was therefore evident that the temperature, to which eggs might be exposed in an incubator, might vary from 96° or 98° to 106° (the temperature of the hen's breast) without danger. Before this experiment was made, the author had assumed that the variation of temperature should not exceed two degrees ; and the first system of regulation used successfully by him (by means of the methylene thermometer and an electro-magnetic detent mechanism controlling a valve engine), could be readily adjusted to maintain the heat within one degree (in either direction) of any desired mean temperature, as proved by a registering thermometer. The experiments with an egg under a hen, and other facts, led him to the conclusion that such excessive nicety was useless. It was also known that eggs had been hatched successfully by keeping the egg in contact with the human body ; and, as the temperature of this rarely exceeds 98°, that temperature must be high enough. Conse-

quently with incubators now made by the author,
no attempt is made to maintain the temperature
more regularly than between 98° and 103°; and this
is found sufficient for all practical purposes. The
mean temperature of the contents of an egg under
such circumstances is about 101°, rising sometimes
to 102° ; which is hotter than the above-mentioned
experiment demonstrated to be the case with an egg
under a hen. There is no doubt that a fresh egg
will hatch a little faster, if the temperature be maintained closely to 102°, than it will if the temperature
be permitted to vary down to 96° or 98° ; the hasten-
ing sometimes being as much as thirty-six hours ;
but as eggs hatched in the natural way require an
average of twenty-one days for the work, and as a
temperature oscillating between 98° and 103° will
bring out the chickens from fresh eggs in from
twenty to twenty-one days, there is no necessity for
greater uniformity.

Incubators made by the author are provided with
a thermometer whose bulb is on about a level with
the middles of the eggs. The highest temperature
denoted by these thermometers should not as a general rule exceed 107°, and need not be more than
102° ; while the lowest should not be below 97°, unless when the drawers are open, or some unusual
occurrence takes place. An occasional rise of temperature in the drawers to 110° will not destroy life
in an egg, provided this temperature be not maintained too long ; and an occasional descent below
90° is not fatal ; if in both cases there be good ventilation and sufficient moisture in the air, as is

always the case with the thermostatic incubator hereafter described.

In addition to the peculiar systems of descending ventilation, heat regulation, and moisture supply devised by the author, he has invented several improvements in the construction of thermostats which are important as rendering their operation more certain and more delicate. One of these consists of the combination of two compound thermostatic bars with one multiplying lever, the fulcrum pivot of which is carried by one of the thermostatic bars. This combination enables about double the amount of movement for regulation to be obtained with thermostatic bars of the same length as compared with the common system of levers. Another improvement is the counterpoising of the weight of the compound thermostatic bars, so as to leave practically their whole expansive force available for regulation. Another improvement is a shifting weight, which is operated by the valve engine and aids the movement of the thermostat alternately in opposite directions, thus counterbalancing the frictional resistance of the regulator detent. These improvements enable the thermostat to regulate the heat with certainty within about one degree of either side of a given mean temperature as tested by a delicate thermometer notwithstanding rapid variations in the supply of heat.

Another improvement devised by the author has reference to the turning of the eggs automatically. As early as 1875 this subject engaged his attention, and in January, 1876, several plans of accomplishing the work were invented. These plans were all based upon the principle of turning the eggs by the frictional contact of their surfaces with those of rollers, or of belts, upon which the eggs rest ; and a patent, dated February 3d, 1880, No. 224,224, has been granted to the author for this system. The best mode of embodying it is to construct the egg holders or egg drawers with a series of parallel rollers, whose journals are supported in bearings secured in the front and back of the drawer ; the axes of the rollers being about two inches apart, and the rollers being one inch in diameter. The rollers are connected by bands, so that when one roller is turned, the whole set turn in the same direction. Hence an egg laid upon any two rollers is caused to turn by the frictional contact of its shell with the surfaces of the rollers. One of the rollers is fitted with a toothed ring, to which the hand is applied if the turning is to be done by hand. If the turning is to be effected automatically, one of the journals is fitted with a ratchet-wheel, and a reciprocating pawl is fitted to act upon the teeth of this wheel. The pawl is operated by clock-work having the ordinary time movement and also a turning movement similar to the striking movement of an ordinary striking clock, but moving the pawl instead of the bell hammer ; so that at any desired interval of time, say every half hour, the time movement of the clock releases the turning movement, and lets the pawl turn the ratchet-wheel and supporting rollers, one or more teeth. In place of using special clock-work, the pawl may be connected either with the valve engine of the incubator, or with a shaft

worked with a special weight, but connected by a
detent with the valve engine ; so that at every alter-
nation of temperature, the eggs may be partially
turned. The eggs will thus be turned progressively,
and a complete revolution may be effected in about
six hours, more or less as deemed expedient. In
place of turning the eggs continually in the same
direction, two ratchet-wheels may be used with a
reversible pawl, or with alternating pawls ; so that
the eggs may be turned alternately in opposite
directions.

An incubator embodying all the author's inven-
tions thus far described, proved to be too expensive
a machine for common use, hence the attempt was
made to simplify its construction without materially
affecting its efficiency. This attempt led to a series
of experiments resulting in the form of incubator described hereafter, and in certain additional improvements for which patents have been granted. This
incubator is described in the following pages ; it holds
160 eggs, and can be sold at a moderate price. In
it the new style of thermostat, invented by the
author and operating by tension, is employed to determine the temperature at which the valves of the
waste heat chimneys are to be opened and closed by
a weight, like a clock weight ; the thermostatic bar
being subjected to a heavy tensile strain by which
the tendency to spring and operate irregularly is
practically done away with. The valve engine is a
strong piece of mechanism without a single cog-
wheel ; all of its members, including the liquid speed
controller, being secured in a strong brass frame,
and being protected from dust by a glass shade.

This incubator can be managed by any person who is competent to operate a sewing-machine or to take care of a clock ; and it can be operated in any room in a house, as with ordinary care an egg need never be broken in it, and need never become offensive. As this incubator has been thoroughly tested, it is confidently offered to those who wish to raise chickens for either profit or amusement.

ROLLER EGG DRAWER.

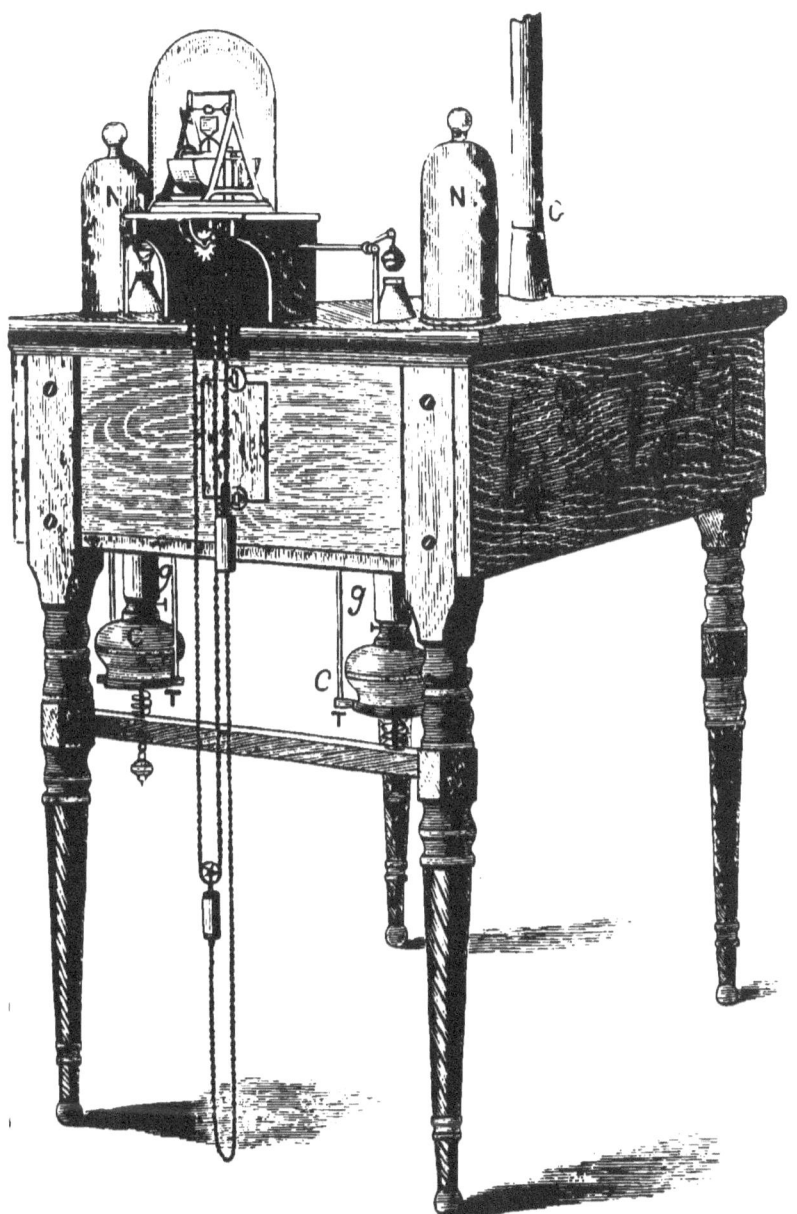

FIG. I.

CONSTRUCTION OF THE INCUBATOR.

THE Thermostatic Incubator in its present form has a capacity of 160 eggs. It is represented in Figs. 1 to 8 inclusive, Fig. 1 being a perspective view of it. Fig. 2 is a horizontal section of it above the egg trays. Fig. 3 is a vertical longitudinal section of the incubator through one of the waste heat chimneys. Fig. 4 is a plan of the incubator with the top removed. Fig. 5 is a central vertical longitudinal section of the incubator. Fig. 6 is a view of the end at which the valve engine is arranged. Figs. 7 and 8 are views of the valve engine of about two fifths of the working dimensions. The same letters are used to indicate the same parts in the various figures.

The incubator comprises the following principal parts—viz. :

1st. The incubating chamber, which is the interior A A' of the main case.

2d. The egg holders B B', which are the drawers or sliding trays at the front and rear of the apparatus. Each of these will hold, without crowding, 40 eggs, which are laid in rows. If the eggs are crowded together, the drawers will hold a larger number, but crowding interferes with the turning of the eggs. The bottom of each drawer is composed of rollers upon which the eggs lie, and which are connected by elastic bands, so that when one roller

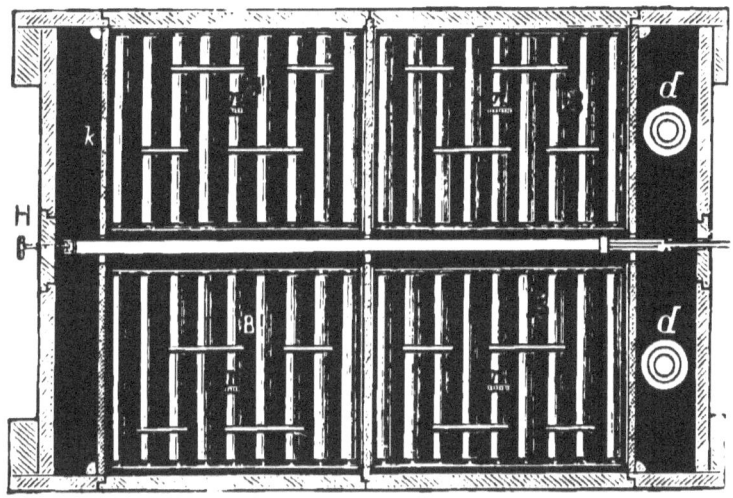

FIG. 2.

is turned all revolve equally and compel the eggs to turn. Hence all the eggs in one drawer can be turned simultaneously by a slight movement of the hand applied from beneath to a stud-wheel n ; the drawer being first partly drawn out of the incubator. This construction of egg holders with rollers was patented to the author February 3d, 1880, (Patent No. 224,224), and he is the only person who

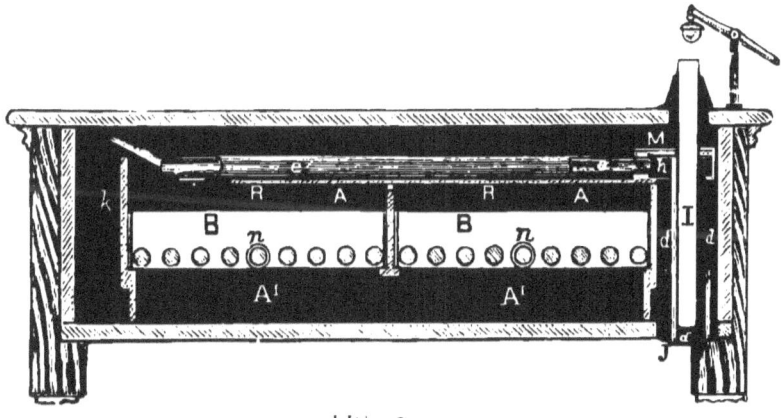

FIG. 3.

is authorized by law to use it or to permit others to do so.

3d. The heat flues *d d*. In the author's first incubators these were at opposite ends of the incubator, but in those now made the heat flues are both at one end of the incubator, this arrangement being in many respects the most expedient. Each heat flue projects below the bottom of the incubating chamber, so that the projecting end may be engaged in the short chimney *g* of a lamp C. Each flue rises to the upper part A of the incubating chamber (A A'), where it passes into a box *h* in an evaporating pan M. From this pan the flue *e e'* extends horizontally toward the opposite end of the incubating chamber, where it is fitted with a vent pipe *a*, which passes into the ventilating chimney. The horizontal portion, *e'*, of the flue is broad and thin, and becomes broader as it recedes from the lamp, so as to present a radiating surface which increases in size as the heat of the gases from the lamp diminishes.

4th. The lamps C C, by which the heat is supplied. These have ordinary kerosene burners and short tin chimneys *g*, each fitted with a pane of mica to permit the flame to be inspected. The lamps are trimmed and filled in the common way. Each lamp is supported upon a movable spring lamp gallery T, which can be depressed to disengage the lamp chimney from the flue above. To remove the lamp for filling and trimming, the operator should grasp the lamp font with one hand and should pull the gallery downward with the other hand sufficiently to disengage the lamp chimney from the flue

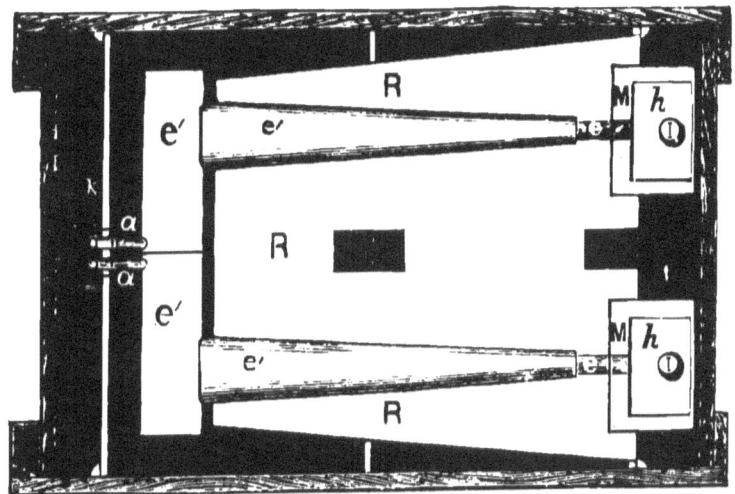

FIG. 4.

above it ; then he should lift the lamp out of the cavity of the gallery and draw it toward him, after which the lamp gallery should be allowed to rise

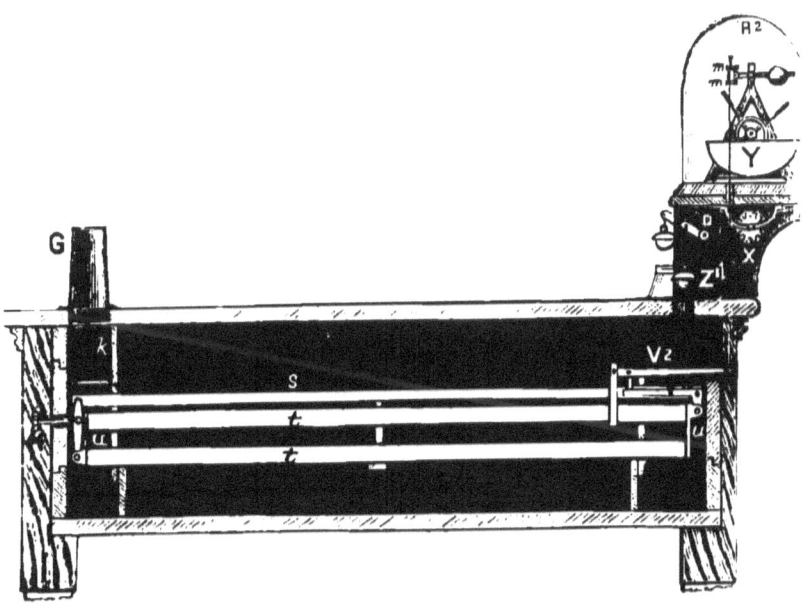

FIG. 5.

gently. The wick should be trimmed slightly rounding. When the lamp is filled, trimmed, and lighted, it may be replaced in the cavity of the lamp gallery, which should be drawn down for the purpose, by applying one hand to the knob pendant of the gallery, sufficiently to permit the short lamp chimney to pass beneath the heat flue ; and when the lamp font is engaged in the gallery, the latter should be permitted to rise slowly by the force of the spring, while the font is steadied by the hand so as to guide the short chimney over the end of the heat flue. The short chimney should be put on with its mica pane outward, so that the height of the flame can be observed.

The lamp fonts are purposely made of large size, so that they will hold kerosene enough for forty-eight hours, in case the operator should some day forget to fill them. The size of the lamp burners depends upon the temperature of the room in which the incubator is used. If the temperature of the room does not sink lower than 65° Fahrenheit, the ordinary "A" burners may be used with advantage. If, however, the temperature of the room is liable to run down below 65° Fahrenheit, "B" burners should be used ; care being taken that the wicks are not turned up too high. The lamp fonts will admit of the use of burners of either size, reducing rings being used to accommodate the rings of the fonts to the dimensions of the screws of "A" burners. The only objection to the use of the larger ("B") burners at all times is the risk of burning more kerosene than is necessary, and the consequent waste of oil. If, however, care be exercised in the adjustment of the wicks, a little practice will enable the operator to use the " B" burners without waste of

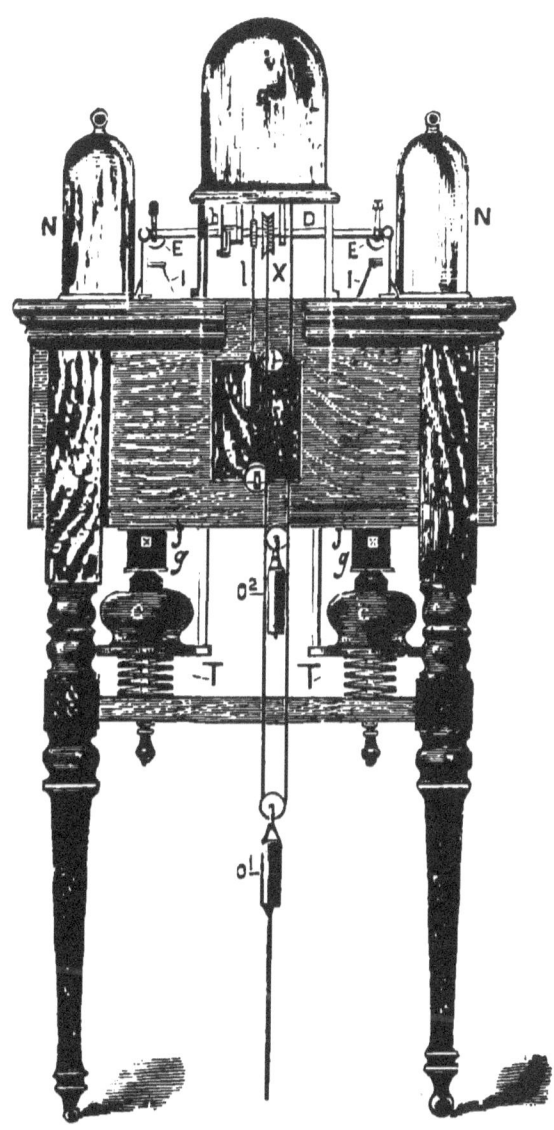

FIG. 6.

oil, whether the room be warm or cold ; but if the incubator be put at work in this latitude during the winter, it is safer to start with B burners and to change the burners when the warm weather in May commences.

5th. The waste heat chimneys I I. There is one of these for each lamp ; each chimney extending through the lamp flue, and passing out of the top of the incubator, where the chimney is fitted with an acorn-shaped drop valve E. When this valve is lowered, the chimney is closed, the waste of heat is prevented, and the heated gases from the lamp are compelled to pass through the lamp flues d, e e', and to heat the incubator. When the valves are raised, the waste heat chimneys are open, and the greater part of the heat from the lamps escapes, thus permitting the incubator to cool.

Hence the opening or closing of the valves of the waste heat chimneys determines the heat of the incubator ; and this opening and closing is effected automatically by the valve engine as controlled by the thermostat.

6th. The air supply pipes for fresh air. There is one of these, J, surrounding each lamp flue d. The fresh air from the air supply pipes is discharged into the upper part of the incubating chamber beneath the evaporating pans M ; and the air is heated as it rises, by the radiation of heat from the upright lamp flues d.

7th. The ventilating chimney G. This is located at the end of the incubator which is furthest from the lamps. A part of it is within the casing, being formed by the partition k ; the residue projects above the top of the incubating chamber.

The ventilating chimney connects by openings

through the lower part of the partition k, with the incubating chamber beneath the perforated bottoms of the egg holders or trays. Hence while the hot air enters at the top of the incubating chamber at one end of it, the foul or colder air passes into the ventilating chimney from the bottom of the opposite end of the chamber, and consequently there is a downward circulation of the heated air through the egg holders and incubating chamber. This downward circulation (as previously explained) tends to equalize the temperature in horizontal directions, while it causes the upper sides of the eggs to be hotter than their under sides, thus corresponding with the application of heat from the body of a hen in natural incubation.

The ventilating chimney also receives the spent gases from the vent pipes a of the heat flues, so that it is always kept warm by such gases, and consequently has a good draught. If, however, the draught should not prove sufficiently active in hot weather (when but a comparatively small quantity of heat is furnished by the lamps) to insure the requisite circulation of air, a piece of pipe two feet in length may be applied to the upper end of the ventilating chimney so as to lengthen it.

In the first incubators made by the author, the base of the part of the ventilating chimney above the incubating chamber was enlarged to receive a valve, which being operated by the valve engine controlled the ventilation automatically. In the incubators as now made by the author, the ventilating valve (z', Figs. 5 and 7) is arranged at the end of the incubator nearest the valve engine, where it is operated directly by the same rock shaft, D, that works the waste heat chimney valves E, being opened and closed simultaneously with them. The opening of this ventilating valve produces supplementary ventilation, and by letting the hottest air escape, prevents possible overheating ; but the valve permits only a partial escape of the heated air, so that the circulation through the incubating chamber is continued, notwithstanding the opening of this ventilating valve.

8th. The evaporators. These consist of two pans (M M, Figs. 3 and 4), located in the upper part of the incubating chamber at the heads of the upright portions of the heat flues d d. Their office is to supply moisture to the air, thus preventing the drying of the eggs. Each evaporator is supplied by a font, N, Figs. 1 and 6, having a feed pipe projecting from its bottom and passing downward, through a hole in the top of the incubator, into its appropriate evaporating pan. The feed pipe of each font is fitted with an automatic ball valve which prevents the escape of water while the font is being withdrawn and replaced. When a font is to be filled, it should be quickly raised with one hand and moved over a shallow pan or a saucer so that any drip may be caught. Then the forefinger of the other hand should be applied to the nozzle of the feed pipe, and the font should be turned upside down and rested upon its head. It may then be readily filled by means of a pitcher and a funnel. After it has been filled, the forefinger of one hand should be applied to the nozzle before the font is turned head upward ; and after it has been turned, it should be held momentarily over the pan or saucer, to catch any drip after the finger is withdrawn from the nozzle. The font may then have its nozzle entered in the hole in the top of the incubator, and should be lowered to its place. As the font descends, the ball valve is opened by a pin secured to the evaporating pan, and the water escapes whenever the level of the water in the evaporating pan sinks low enough to unseal the nozzle of the font.

9th. The heat distributor. As the lamps and the evaporators are both at the same end of the incubator, and as the heat of the flues must therefore be progressively less as they extend toward the opposite end, while the air admitted for ventilation also tends to cool down in its passage from the vicinity of the evaporators onward and downward to the lower end of the ventilating chimney, the incubator should be hottest near the lamps, and the heat should be progressively lower toward the ventilating chimney. This is the natural tendency ; and to obviate it, the heat distributer R is provided. This distributer consists of a diaphragm of pasteboard, or other material, arranged horizontally between the under sides of the horizontal flues *e e'*, and the open tops of the egg holders beneath. The diaphragm is partly cut away so as to permit the descent of the warm air and the moisture carried by it ; and the removal of portions by cutting away is greatest over the drawers which are furthest from the lamps. The operation of this distributer is to obstruct the direct downward passage of all the warm air through the drawers that are nearest the lamps ; to cause a

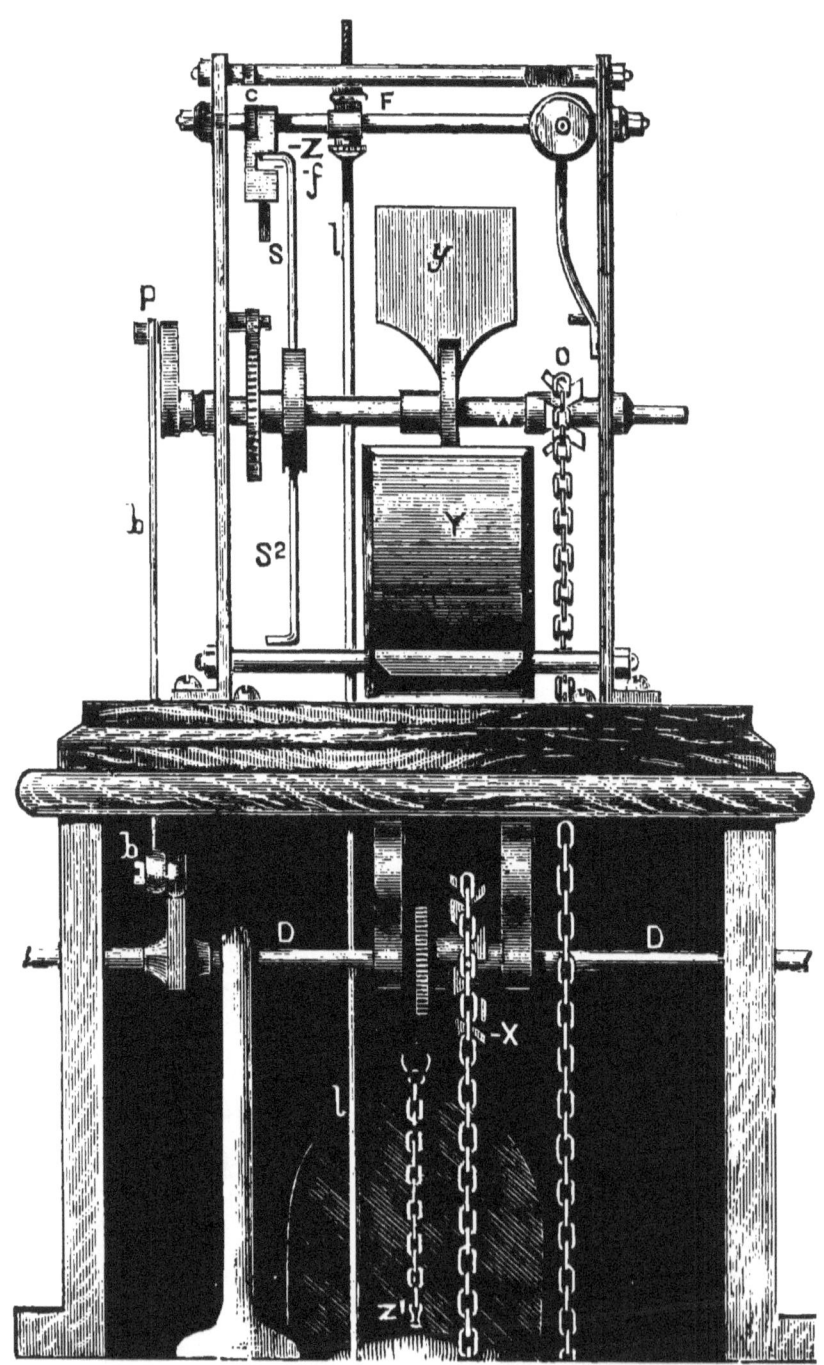

FIG. 7.

large portion of the hot air to move along over the
distributer to the drawers that are farthest from the
lamps ; to obstruct the direct radiation of heat from
the portions of the horizontal flues *ce'* that are nearest
the lamps ; and by the above operations to distribute the heat more equally than it would be other-
wise. The substance which we prefer to use as the
material for the heat distributer is what is commonly called heavy tar-board, which is a pasteboard
made from tarred junk, and it is thoroughly varnished with shellac varnish to repel moisture.

10th. The valve engine. This engine is represented more fully in Figs. 7 and 8. It is mounted
upon a pedestal at the top of the apparatus, and is
covered by a removable glass shade R'. Its main
shaft W, Fig. 7, is fitted at one end with a crank P,
whose wrist pin is connected by means of a connecting rod *b* with an arm projecting from the valve
shaft (D, Figs. 5, 6 and 7) beneath the valve engine.
This valve shaft extends across the top of the incubator and is fitted at its ends with arms from which
the drop valves E are suspended. The weight of
the valves and arms of this rock-shaft is counterpoised, so that a very small force is required to move
the valves.

The valve engine is driven by a weight hanging
upon a chain which passes round the chain pulley (O,
Fig. 7) on the main shaft W. The chain is endless,
and is divided into two loops by the winding pulley X. Each loop holds a weight ; the larger (*o'*) of
which furnishes the force for driving the engine,
while the lighter weight *o²* tautens the chain. As the
heavier weight runs down in working the valve

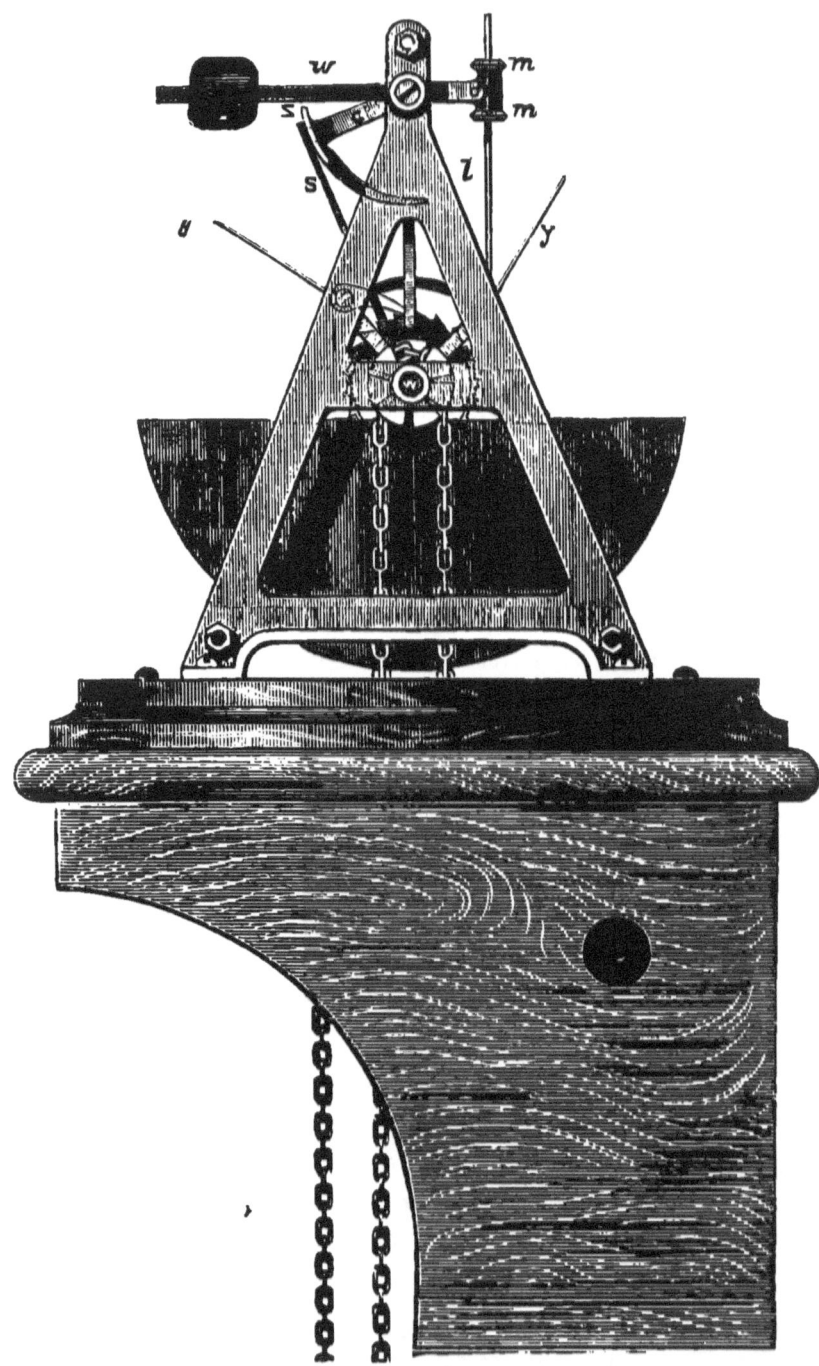

FIG. 8.

engine, the lighter weight is drawn up, and if the heavier weight should be permitted to run down to the floor, the further movement of the valve engine would be prevented. Hence the heavier weight must be wound up periodically, generally every morning and evening. the winding being effected by taking hold of the strand of chain which extends from the lighter weight o^2 (Fig. 6) to the winding pulley X and pulling it downward ; the operation being repeated until the heavier weight is wound up close to the winding pulley. Care must be taken that the loops of chain are not twisted, and are not out of the pulleys of the weights or the winding pulley ; either of which contingencies would render the valve engine inoperative.

The valve engine now used is less sensitive in its action than the most perfect one which the author has produced ; but the loss in sensitiveness is compensated by simplicity, while the sensitiveness is sufficient to cause the engine to operate with a change of 3° of temperature. Those who desire a detailed description of a valve engine so sensitive that it will operate with a change of half a degree of temperature, will find it in the author's American patent, No. 210,559, dated December 3d, 1878, a printed copy of which may be procured from the Patent Office.

11th. The speed controller. This consists of a four-armed paddle-wheel y, Figs. 5, 7. and 8, revolving in a trough Y containing a liquid. Its office is to prevent the valve engine from moving too rapidly and stopping with a jar. The trough should be filled with oil or glycerine up to within about three quarters of an inch of its brim, and the liquid should not be allowed to become thick. The best liquid for the purpose is a mixture of about equal quantities of water and glycerine, with the addition of about a teaspoonful of carbolic acid to prevent putrefaction. This mixture rarely requires replenishing. The liquid prevents the rapid movement of the paddle-wheel; and as the paddle-wheel is secured to the main shaft of the valve engine, the speed of the latter is controlled, although the force of the driving weight is considerably in excess of that required to move the valves.

The mode in which the valve engine operates is as follows: Above the main shaft W there is a rock shaft F, which carries a lever c, having at one end a curved plate Z. The main shaft is provided with arms S S^2 (hereafter more fully described), which alternately come in contact with the slotted curved plate Z, called the detent. The heavier weight o' tends continually to cause the main shaft to revolve; but this revolution is alternately permitted and stopped by the action of the detent Z, whose position, as hereafter described, is determined by the Thermostat. Whenever the main shaft revolves, it carries with it the crank P. If the crank is thereby turned half a revolution from its lowermost to its uppermost position, the rock shaft D is rocked to drop the drop valves E E, thereby forcing the heat from the lamps to pass through the flues and raise the temperature of the incubator. When, on the other hand, the crank P is turned half a revolution from its highest to its lowest position, the rock shaft D is rocked to raise the drop valves F, thereby allowing the heat from the lamps to escape, the result of which is the cooling of the incubator until the next operation of the valve engine.

12th. The thermostat. This is a species of thermometer using the expansion of a solid in place of the expansion of a liquid to indicate variations of temperature. The first thermostat used by the author was a compound bar composed of two strips of vulcanite and brass riveted together, and various improvements were devised to render the implement sensitive and certain in its action. The thermostat now used, while sufficiently sensitive in its action, can be afforded at a less price than the compound bar, and its construction is based upon the different longitudinal expansions of vulcanite and dry wood or equivalent material. It consists of a strip of vulcanite s, Fig. 5, strained longitudinally upon a frame composed of two wooden bars t t, and of the metallic connections u of those bars. The strip is about thirty-nine inches long, and the difference in expansion between it and the wooden bars is multiplied by two levers V' V², the last of which is connected by a rod l with the lever arm w of the detent Z of the valve engine. The weight of the longer arms of the levers and of the rod l is more than counterpoised by the weight U, so that the strip of vulcanite is constantly under longitudinal tension, and the play or loose fitting of all the connections is taken up. The thermostat is set in the middle of the incubator between the backs of the front and rear drawers or trays, so that it is exposed to the variations of temperature which affect the eggs. The longitudinal expansion of the vulcanite by an increase of heat in the incubating chamber permits the weight U to move the detent Z of the valve engine downward ; and the contraction of the strip incident to a decrease of heat raises the weight U, and moves the same detent upward.

The mode in which the detent controls the move-ment of the valve engine is as follows : The main shaft of the engine is provided with two detent arms S S², Figs. 7 and 8, the end of each of which is bent horizontally and is fitted to bear against the curved plate of the detent Z. At the central part of this curved plate there is a slot f large enough to permit the bent end of either detent arm to pass freely ; but when the slot does not correspond with the position of the bent end of the detent arm, the movement of the latter is stopped by contact with the curved plate of the detent against which the arm then rests. The detent arms are diametrically opposite each other, but their bent ends are at different distances from the centre of the main shaft W, from which they project ; the difference in dis-tance being such that if the detent be in the position to permit one of the arms to pass through its slot, the opposite detent arm, after making half of a revolu-tion with the main shaft W, will have its movement stopped by contact with the surface of the detent plate. If such stoppage should occur when the bent end of the longer detent arm comes in contact with the detent Z, the valve engine will remain at rest, notwithstanding the effort of the weight to turn the main shaft, until the heat in the incubating chambers falls and the consequent contraction of the thermostat pulls the detent plate upward and brings its central slot opposite the bent end of the detent arm, thus freeing it and permitting the main shaft to turn and close the drop valves. This operation requires half a revolution and brings the shorter detent arm to the detent plate, the slot of which, however, does not now correspond with that arm. Hence, the further movement of the shorter detent arm will be prevented, and the valve engine will remain at rest until the heat rises sufficiently to expand the thermostat and let the detent be moved downward by the weight until its slot comes oppo- site the bent end of the shorter detent arm, and releases it ; whereupon the valve engine will be per- mitted to make a second half of a revolution, and so to open the drop valves.

The relative differences of the lengths of the de- tent arms and the width of the slot in the detent de- termine the variation in temperature which is per- mitted, and the apparatus is permanently adjusted to operate with a variation of about 3° Fahrenheit. The highest temperature to be attained is adjust- able by the user ; and two means of adjustment are provided, either or both of which may be used as found expedient. One of these means is the screw H (Fig. 5) by which one end of the vul- canite strip of the thermostat is held in place. The milled head of this adjusting screw is at the outside of the end of the incubator that is farthest from the lamps, and it moves a lever with which the end of the vulcanite strip of the thermostat is connected. The turning of the upper edge of this screw head to the right hand has the same effect upon the multiply- ing levers as a reduction of temperature ; and the turning of the same screw head to the left hand has the same effect as a rise in temperature. As this adjusting screw operates almost directly upon the vulcanite, its movement provides for large adjustments of temperature.

The second means of adjustment consists of adjusting nuts *m* applied to the screwed upper end of the rod *l*, Fig. 8. The upper of these nuts only is necessary, as the lower nut may be left a short distance below the sleeve connection with the detent. If the temperature of the incubator is to run higher, the upper adjusting nut *m* is to be screwed higher on the rod *l ;* and if the temperature is to run lower, the upper nut is to be screwed downward on the rod. If the lower nut is used, it must be screwed upward after the upper nut is moved, and must be screwed downward before the upper nut is moved. This second means of adjustment provides for small adjustments of temperature, and for any swelling and contraction of the case of the incubator which may possibly take place.

PREPARATIONS FOR WORK.

THE incubator should be placed in a room in the house, where it will not be exposed to excessive heat or cold, nor to drafts of air. The incubator may be used in any room occupied for other purposes, as when ordinary care is taken it does not give out any smell or effluvia. The first incubator of the author was operated in his billiard-room, and for seven years past all the chickens have been hatched in the house ; the incubator being in charge of the gardener, who comes in for a few minutes, morning and evening, to attend to it.

Before starting the incubator, the valve connections should be examined for the purpose of ascertaining whether the valves are in a condition to move freely. The valve shaft should always have a little play endwise, so as to prevent binding. It should be noticed whether the valves when lowered do or do not drop fairly into the heads of the waste heat chimneys. If they do not, the screws which secure the heads of the waste heat chimneys to the top of the incubator may be slacked, and the heads may be moved to suit the valves, after which the screws should be retightened.

The paddles of the liquid speed controller should be examined for the purpose of ascertaining whether they turn freely in the trough. The arms may have been bent, in which case they should be bent back ;

or the trough may have been displaced by the jars of transportation, and its sides may bind against the paddles. In such cases the sides of the trough may be slightly bent, or the screws that secure the trough to the frame of the valve engine should be slacked and the trough moved sufficiently to free its sides from the paddles, after which the screws should be retightened.

The bearings of the valve engine and weight pulleys should be oiled with sewing-machine oil, or (better) with clock oil ; as well as the face of the curved detent plate. An extremely small quantity of oil is required for this purpose, as may be judged from the fact that a single fluid ounce served the author six years. The oil is most readily applied by dipping the end of a piece of small wire in the oil, and transferring the minute drop to the bearing.

The trough of the speed controller should be filled with water, or with the mixture of glycerine and water previously mentioned, to within about three quarters of an inch of its brim.

The freedom of the valve engine and valves should be tested by causing the regulator detent (Z, Figs. 7, 8) to move up and down by turning the adjusting screw H, Fig. 5, in alternately opposite directions, so as to release the two regulator detent arms successively ; the weight being permitted to work the engine and valves after each movement. If the valves do not open and close regularly, something binds which requires adjustment.

When the engine and valves are found to operate properly, the lamps may be filled and lighted, and the glass water fonts may be filled with water and put in place ; the adjusting screw being so turned that the valves remain closed, with the detent slot about an inch above the end of the detent arm.

The lamp wicks should be turned up after the lamps are in place, slightly at first, and farther as the flues become warm and the draught improves, care being taken that the wicks are never turned up so high that the lamps smoke. The height of the flame to be used depends upon the temperature of the room in which the incubator is used. As a general rule, the flame should be of such a height that the valves will open and close on the average about two or three times an hour when the apparatus is in working order. If the wicks are trimmed properly, flames of B burners of about three eights of an inch in height above the cones or deflectors of the lamps will answer, when in the spring of the year the temperature of the room varies from 50° to 70°. In summer the flames should be lower than in spring ; but the best adjustment can be learned only by practice. When the incubator is started, it takes some time to heat up, and when the temperature rises to 100° in the drawers, the wicks can be readjusted as found expedient. As the incubator heats up, the detent will be lowered by the expansion of the thermostat, and if it should be so lowered that the slot of the detent approaches the detent arm before the temperature reaches 100°, the regulator screw should be turned to raise the detent higher, so that when the temperature reaches 102°, the detent slot permits the arm to pass through it.

The lamp wicks should be trimmed rounding.

The kerosene used should be of the best quality, such, for example, as Devoe's Brilliant Oil, because poor kerosene causes the rapid crusting of the lamp wicks, and the consequent variation of the heat. If the kerosene be good, the lamps require to be trimmed but once in twenty-four hours, and then but slightly ; in fact, what little crust there is can be rubbed off with a piece of paper. The quantity of kerosene used depends greatly upon the skill of the attendant in adjusting the wicks ; but the proper adjustment is speedily learned by practice. If, for example, the incubator is used in a room which is cooler during the night than in the day-time, the lamp wicks should be turned slightly higher in the evening than they are set in the morning.

When the incubator is first put at work by an inexperienced operator, it should be allowed to run several days before eggs are put into it, so that the operator may become familiar with its management.

The interior of the incubator may be examined by removing the top. The following operations are required for this purpose. The connecting rod (*l*, Figs. 7, 8), between the valve engine and thermostat, must be disconnected at its lower end from the lever V* of the thermostat, and from the valve engine at its upper end, and must be lifted out. The water fonts should be lifted off. The screws, which hold the heads of the waste heat chimneys in place, must be taken out, and the waste heat chimneys lifted out of the holes in the heads. This may be readily done when the valves are open or raised, by canting the chimney heads sidewise as they are lifted. The thermometer must also be lifted out.

care being taken to raise with it the pieces of cork which hold it in place. The chain and weights of the valve engine must be drawn up and laid upon the top of the incubator. The screws which secure the top of the incubator may then be taken out, and the top lifted off.

The disconnection of the connecting rod *l* may be effected as follows : Apply the forefinger of the left hand beneath the end of the uppermost lever of the thermostat, which projects through the hole in the end door under the valve engine. The rod above the lever should be seized with the thumb and forefinger of the right hand, and should be pulled downward and slightly outward, so as to disengage the hooked lower end of the rod from the pivot of the lever. When the hook is disengaged, the rod may be permitted to move upward by the pull of the counterpoise of the valve engine. Afterward, the pivot which connects the upper end of the rod *l* with the shank of the detent, should be removed, and while the rod is held by the left hand, the rod should be drawn upward. The rod may be replaced by reversing the above operations, taking care that the opening of the hook at the lower end of the rod faces toward the end of the incubator.

When the top of the incubator is off, the distributer R should be examined for fear it may have been displaced by transportation, although such an accident is not likely to happen. When the distributer is in its proper position, one end of it should be attached to the partition beneath the evaporators, and the edges of its sides should be equidistant from the front and rear of the incubator.

WHEN but one incubator is employed for hatching chickens for domestic use, it is not the best plan to have too many of the same age hatched at a time; besides, when but few hens are kept, it is not always easy to procure the requisite number of fresh eggs, of the kind wanted, to fill the incubator at one operation. Hence, when starting the incubator for domestic use, it is expedient to put in only about two or three dozens of eggs, and to put in two additional dozens every second or third day until the trays are full.

Before the eggs are put in, it is expedient to mark them with the date. This may be done with a pen and ink as follows: Hold the egg in the left hand against the rim of a table, or other support, such as a book laid on a table, on which the right arm is sustained, and mark the egg thus:

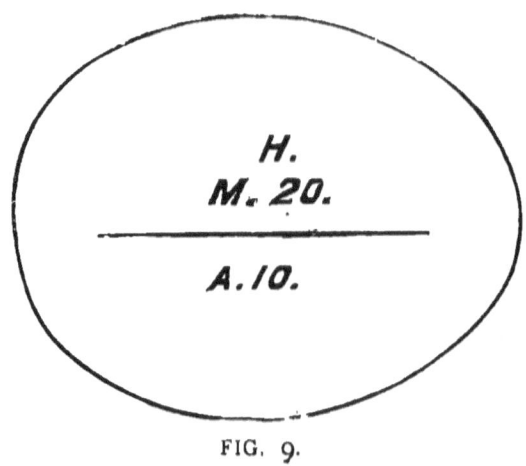

FIG. 9.

The first letter may be the designation of the pen or breed ; thus, H may designate Houdan ; L, Leghorn ; L. B. Light Brahma, etc.

The second line of letters and number denotes the month and day when the eggs are put into the incubator, say March 20th.

The lowest letter and number denote a date three weeks later, being the date upon which the chickens are expected, say April 10th.

The straight line between the dates shows the part of the egg that is to be uppermost during the day.

As fast as the eggs are thus marked, place them in a shallow tray, pan, or paper box, having its bottom set at a slight slant so as to prevent rolling. When the marks are dry, take up each egg with the left hand, and with the inscription uppermost ; turn it over endwise between the forefinger and thumb as pivots, so as to bring uppermost the side directly opposite the inscription, and mark this side with a single line, thus :

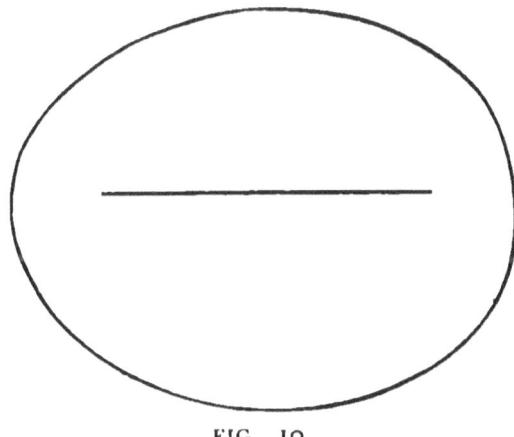

FIG. 10.

This line (unaccompanied by any date) indicates the side of the egg that is to be turned uppermost at night.

These marks render the turning of the eggs with substantial accuracy a very easy and rapid operation ; besides always indicating the time when the chickens may be expected, and furnishing an index of the state of incubation.

The incubator should be attended to twice a day ; viz., early in the morning, and about ten or twelve hours afterward in the evening. The attendance in the morning should be,

1. The registration of the temperature of every thermometer enclosed in the incubator, and particularly of the highest and lowest temperatures indicated by a registering thermometer, which, if not provided with the incubator, should be placed in the middle of one of the drawers upon two wooden blocks, so that its bulb is about level with the upper sides of the eggs.

2. The turning of the eggs half round, which is effected by opening the front or flap of each tray, drawing the tray partially outward so that its contents may be seen, and turning the stud ring on the middle roller until the marks upon the under sides of the eggs are turned uppermost.

3. The filling of the water fonts, and of the trough of the speed controller in case water be used in it. If oil, or a mixture of water and glycerine be used, the trough of the speed controller rarely requires attention.

4. The winding of the weight of the valve engine.

5. The filling and trimming of the lamps. The

advantage of doing this work last is that it obviates the risk of having kerosene on the hands when handling the eggs or filling the fonts.

At night, the same work is to be done with the exception of filling the water bottles and trimming the lamps, unless the wicks have become crusted by the use of poor kerosene. If, however, the room is very cool at night, or liable to become so, the lamps should be turned up slightly higher than for the day-time. If the registering thermometer is in a drawer or is inside the incubator, then, about half an hour after the drawers have been opened, the indexes of the thermometer should be reset, unless the drawer has been kept open so short a time that the temperature at closing it is between 100° and 103°, in which case the indexes may be set at once.

When trays are used which are not provided with means for turning the eggs simultaneously, the eggs should be turned by hand as rapidly as practicable, commencing with the eggs that are nearest the back of the drawer or tray ; and, as the work proceeds, the tray should be progressively shoved in. In fact, the less the drawers or trays are opened, and the shorter the time during which they are kept open, the more equable will be the heat, and the less will the operation of incubation be affected. As the ventilation of the thermostatic incubator is automatic and practically perfect, it is unnecessary to expose the eggs to cool air by keeping the drawers open, unless some accident has occurred which has caused the overheating of the eggs.

The valve-engine should be oiled occasionally, say about once a week. This operation is performed

most readily by means of a piece of broom corn, or
a piece of fine wire, the point of which is dipped
into a vessel of oil. The minute drop, accumulated
on the point of the instrument, is applied in succession to each bearing of each shaft ; and the face of
the detent and the ends of the two detent arms of
the main shaft also should be oiled by touching them
slightly with the point of the finger slightly
moistened with oil, as all that is required is a greasy
surface ; the detent being held by the left hand
during the operation of thus greasing its face. The
pivots of the chain pulleys of the weights should
also be oiled occasionally. So long as the bearing
surfaces of the engine and pulleys do not become
dry, the less the quantity of oil used the better will
be the result. The engine will run frequently
several weeks without reoiling ; but if a bearing
should happen to become dry and stick, the incubator would cease to regulate, and the eggs might be
spoiled, unless the difficulty should be discovered in
time. Hence it is better to oil the engine at least
once, or even twice, a week, applying the oil as
sparingly as possible, and wiping off any surplus
with a soft rag on the end of a small stick, than to
run any risk of dryness.

It is possible that the temperature in the egg
trays which are furthest from the lamps may run
lower than that of the egg trays which are nearer
the lamps. This contingency is most likely to occur
in hot weather, when from the approximation of the
temperature of the atmosphere to that of the interior of the incubator, the draught becomes sluggish. If there should be a greater difference than

one degree between the mean temperatures in the farther and nearer trays, the matter should be remedied, which is readily done by increasing the length of the ventilating pipe so as to cause the warm air to traverse the incubator more rapidly. Such a larger ventilating pipe of galvanized iron, roofing tin, or zinc may be procured of any tinsmith. Or, a much better pipe may be made by rolling a sheet of common wrapping-paper or of thin pasteboard upon a wooden roller or core two and a half inches in diameter, and pasting all but the inside layer as the rolling progresses. After the paper becomes dry, the pipe should be slit longitudinally with a pen-knife to enable it to be removed from the wooden core, and should then be enveloped in several layers of a sheet of paper covered on one side with paste. The paper pipe should subsequently be varnished.

If the temperature of the room does not exceed 70°, supplementary ventilation through the valve opening of the valve Z' is unnecessary, and the valve may be temporarily rendered inoperative. This may be readily effected by making a cone or cornucopia of paper and pushing it point downward into the valve opening, thus closing it, but permitting the valve to be raised and lowered regularly by the operation of the valve engine.

About the sixth or seventh day after each lot of eggs is put into the incubator, they should be examined by means of an egg tester, and such as are clear should be set aside, as they are not fertile. These unfertile eggs may be boiled at once, and kept for feeding the young chickens. Sometimes an unfertile egg may escape detection, and it is also possible that a partially developed chicken may die in the shell ; hence two days before the eggs are expected to hatch they may be tested by placing them gently, a few at a time, in a large bowl or in a bucket of water heated to 104°. In a short time the eggs which contain live chickens will commence to bob about. The eggs which sink are addled, and those which float without bobbing are either addled from being originally unfertile, or contain germs which have progressed to a certain point and have then died. After the eggs have been tested, the live ones should be replaced in the incubator.

After the last testing of the eggs, they should be placed in trays or drawers having bottoms of perforated metal (two of which are furnished with each of the author's incubators) which should be inserted in the incubator in place of the roller drawers, so that the chickens will have a good surface to stand upon when they emerge from the shells. From the time the eggs are placed in these hatching trays until the chickens peck the shells, the eggs should be turned twice a day by hand.

Or, if preferred, the eggs may remain upon the rollers while the chickens come out of the shells. In this case the chicken drops between the rollers, and will be found under the egg tray, and on the bottom of the incubator. The only objections to this course are that the chicken may possibly be injured in passing between the rollers, and that the rollers and bottom of the incubator are made dirty by the membranes from the eggs and the droppings of the chickens. In such case the rollers should be cleaned before fresh eggs are put upon them ; and coarse paper should be placed on the bottom of the incubator to receive the foul matter, the paper being occasionally changed.

When the shell of an egg is pecked, the pecked side should not be turned downward, for if this be done the chicken will sometimes be smothered by the moisture of the inner membrane of the egg. A pecked egg should be so turned that the pecked part is at the right or left side of the egg. When the chickens are hatching, the eggs should be far enough apart endwise, say at least three quarters of an inch, to allow the chickens to stretch themselves out of the shells ; and the chickens should be left in the tray not less than six hours, or until their feathers become dry ; the egg shells being removed. The chickens may remain in the incubator twelve hours or even twenty-four hours without harm, and often with advantage, although sometimes one will make his way over the top of the tray, and will be found on the bottom of the incubator.

Sometimes a chicken pecks the shell, but from some malformation, or lack of vigor, or from misplacement of the head, is unable to peck a crevice sufficiently round the egg to enable the shell to part. Cases of this kind have never occurred with the author unless the parents were too closely related or too old. When they do occur, the chicken will die unless relief be afforded by opening the shell by hand. As, however, this operation must be performed with great delicacy, in order that the chick may not be wounded, great care must be exercised ; and even then the result will probably be unsuccessful unless the operator is a practised hand. There are two ways of operating in such a case, one or the other of which may be preferable according to circumstances. If the chicken has already pecked the shell, the operator may crush the shell from the pecked opening around the egg in a ring, by means of his thumb nail, and he may then tear the membrane surrounding the chick. If the chick has not pecked the shell at the close of the twenty-second day, the shell may be opened, by means of a sharp-pointed implement, at about the distance from the large end at which the shell is usually pecked. The best implement for the purpose is the point of a pen-knife or the point of the tang of a small file. The point of the instrument should be engaged in the hole of the shell to the least possible extent and be pryed outward so as to break out a minute piece of shell. By a succession of such operations, a ring crevice can be formed which, upon breaking the membrane, will permit the chicken to escape.

Sometimes chickens are weak in the legs when first hatched, so that they cannot stand upright even at the end of five or six hours, but lay on their bellies with their legs sprawled out sidewise. This weakness generally arises from too close in-breeding, as we have never noticed it in chickens that are from parents which are not related, or are but distantly related. Such chickens generally die when hatched by a hen ; and when they are hatched by an incubator they will not generally be of any value if left without treatment. The trouble can be readily cured by connecting the legs loosely by means of a piece of soft cord or woollen yarn. The easiest way to manage the matter is to let one person hold the chicken with its belly upward, while another does the tying. A separate piece of yarn is tied loosely around each leg, below the hock joint ; then the long ends of the two pieces are tied together, leaving the hock joints about three quarters of an inch apart. After the tying is completed, all the loose ends of the yarn should be cut off with a scissors to within a quarter of an inch of the knots. Chickens treated in this way are able to walk and get their food, and after a few days they become so strong that the yarns may be cut off.

If ordinary care be exercised, a bad egg need never be broken in the incubator, because before such eggs burst, they either smell badly, or they exude beads of matter through the pores of the shell, or their shells split longitudinally without breaking the membrane within. Hence, if the eggs are looked at morning and evening, and the operator has a sensitive nose, an addled egg can generally be detected and removed. If, however, an egg should be broken, such eggs as have been spattered by the contents of the broken one should be at once washed in lukewarm water containing a few drops of carbolic acid. The egg tray should be opened sufficiently to hold a pan under the place where the egg broke, and water containing carbolic acid should be poured through the perforated bottom or upon the rollers of the drawer so as to cleanse them thoroughly. The bottom of the incubator also should be washed with water containing carbolic acid, a sponge being used for the purpose.

If by reason of any accident the heat should rise

as high as 108°, all the drawers or trays should be taken out and set upon the floor until the heat falls to 90° or 95°, and should then be replaced. If the excessive heat has not lasted for too long a period, a heat considerably higher than 108° will not be fatal. Thus, in the course of the author's experiments with different arrangements of valve engines and thermostats, the heat on one occasion ran up to 120°, and must have been in the vicinity of that temperature for nearly an hour ; yet not a single egg had its vitality destroyed, although the incubator contained eggs in all states of incubation ; the probable reasons being that the ample supply of moisture and fresh air enabled the germs to withstand the excessive heat for a short period without destruction of life ; and that as the contents of an egg are bad conductors of heat, the heat within the egg was materially lower than that of the incubating chamber.

When the work of incubation is completed for the season, the fonts should be removed and the water should be withdrawn from the evaporating pans by means of a syphon, the short leg of which is inserted through the holes for the font nozzles. If water containing mineral salts be used for the water fonts, the incessant evaporation will produce a deposit in the evaporating pans, which would be very injurious. The only mode of removing this is to take off the top of the incubator so that the pans may be got at and cleansed. Any rough substance, such as an oyster shell, inserted in the evaporating pan will tend to induce the deposit of the salt upon it ; hence it is a good plan to keep an oyster shell in each evaporating pan if impure water be used. The better plan, however, is to use only clean rain water for filling the water fonts, as this is free from all mineral salts.

The size of lamp burner which is used with the incubator depends upon the temperature of the room in which the incubator is used, and should be changed, if found expedient, as directed under the head of " Construction."

The milled regulating nuts previously described upon the upper end of the rod l for adjusting the operation of the thermostat, or the adjusting screw H, require occasional adjustment. If in the process of progressive adjustment it should be found necessary to screw the milled nuts very near to the upper end of the rod, it would be better to slightly screw up the adjusting screw H at the end of the incubator rather than to screw the milled nuts on the adjusting rod l too high.

It is a remote possibility that the atmosphere of the incubator may not be sufficiently moist to enable the eggs to hatch properly. If, therefore, the heat has not been excessive, and fertile eggs should not hatch, it would be well to ascertain whether the trouble is due to want of moisture. This may be done by sprinkling the eggs in the drawers with warm water, after the eggs have been turned. If this water does not dry within half an hour after the drawer is closed, the fault is not want of moisture. If the water dries rapidly, the sprinkling may be continued once a day, or both morning and evening, without risk, and the result noted. If, thereafter, the eggs hatch better, the difficulty has been want of moisture. During hatching eggs will bear a great deal of moisture without injury ; thus the author has immersed eggs in water for three quarters of their length ; the eggs being sustained upright, with their large ends uppermost, in cellular water trays placed in the incubator, and being kept in the water until the nineteenth day, after which they were put in dry drawers ; and the eggs hatched. If, however, there be so much moisture in the atmosphere of the incubator that it condenses upon the shells of the warm eggs and forms a film of water thereon, the pores of the egg shell will be closed and the germ or partially developed chick will be suffocated ; the death of the egg being generally followed by the longitudinal splitting of the shell from end to end. If, therefore, such splitting of the shell takes place with an egg which has previously been proved to be fertile, and the incubator has not been overheated or has not been too cold, the presumption is that the moisture is in excess in the incubator, and the sprinkling of the eggs should be reduced or discontinued.

Every egg that has been adjudged to be fertile after being tested in an egg tester, and that does not subsequently hatch, should be removed on the twenty-second day and opened for the purpose of ascertaining whether its want of fertility escaped detection or the chick has died subsequently to examination. As such eggs are sometimes offensive, the better way to open them is to drop them upon the ground at arms' length, so that they do not spatter the operator.

The temperature of the incubator may be adjusted

to suit the views of the operator, by means of the adjusting screw and the nuts of the rod *l.* According to the author's experience fertile eggs will hatch with certainty when the highest temperature recorded by the thermometer supplied with the incubator does not exceed 102° F., and the temperature when the incubator is working regularly does not run down regularly below 98°. The temperature at the level of the tops of the eggs may, however, run up to 106°, without material risk. If an examination of the thermometer shows that the temperature has exceeded 102°, it has been the author's practice to adjust the mechanism to open the valves sooner ; a maximum temperature of 103° or 104° at the upper sides of the eggs being sufficient.

The larger the number of eggs in the thermostatic incubator, the more regularly will it run as respects temperature ; and when it contains its full complement of eggs the temperature of the atmosphere within it, when the drawers are closed, will not vary more than 4° as indicated by the thermometer. Under such circumstances the variation of the temperature of the interior of an egg must be very minute. As the presence of a large number of eggs in each drawer or tray tends to keep the temperature more uniform, it is a good plan, when a tray is not at least half full of eggs, to put into it a quantity of porcelain eggs, and to remove them as the space is required for fresh eggs ; or to increase the number of porcelain eggs when fresh eggs are not supplied as fast as chickens are hatched, which is frequently the case toward the close of the hatching season, when the incubator is employed to hatch chickens for family use.

Whether the incubator operates successfully or its use ends in disappointment, it is expedient that a record of every proceeding, incident, and effect should be kept ; for by this means alone is one able to reconsider the work and to ascertain what was needed to have insured success.   Every operator will naturally have his own peculiar views as to the form of his journal.   The author has found it convenient to use one divided by upright lines into columns in which are entered on the same horizontal line, the date ; the hour of observation ; the highest and lowest temperatures of each tray as indicated by a registering thermometer ; the temperature of the room in which the incubator is operated ; the temperature of the vent pipe for foul air ; the number and kinds of eggs put in ; the number and kinds of eggs removed as unfertile ; and the number and kinds of chickens obtained. A note also is made of any unusual occurrence, such as the resetting of the regulator.

In addition to the thermometers above mentioned, it is expedient to have one whose bulb is inclosed in a small tin cylinder of about the same capacity as an egg, the residue of the cylinder being filled with glycerine.   The cylinder should be set in one of the drawers on a level with the eggs.   The indications of such an enclosed thermometer afford a close approximation of the internal temperature of the eggs.

IF proper means be provided, chickens hatched by an incubator can be raised with less expense and trouble, and with less loss, than chickens under the care of hens. This statement is not a speculation, but is the result of the author's experience, and of a comparison of seven years' hatching and raising by hens, with seven years' hatching by means of an incubator, and raising by means of brooders an average of 250 chickens and 40 ducks annually, which is the number required in his family for the larder and for replacing the old stock. The requisites for raising chickens artificially are warmth, ventilation, cleanliness, exercise, green food, and the separation of chickens of different sizes into classes, so that the younger or smaller are not trodden and maltreated by the larger.

In order that the requisite warmth may be supplied, various contrivances called "artificial mothers" have been devised; but this term is a misnomer, as the most essential functions of the hen are not performed, while the name brooder is much more appropriate in view of the purposes for which the devices are employed. The ordinary artificial mothers consist of an inclined board having its under side lined with flannel or sheepskin, enclosed at the ends and at its lowest edge, and set upon a floor. These, however, will not answer if the

weather be cool. Artificial mothers are now furnished by manufacturers in which the inclined board
is replaced by a water heater, through which a lamp
flue is conducted ; and the heat is furnished by a
kerosene lamp.   The author found that such artificial mothers were not sufficiently ventilated.   Hence
he devised a new kind of brooder in which the floor
under the inclined board, or brood-cover, is of perforated metal, and heat and ventilation are simultaneously supplied by a slow current of air which is
warmed by a lamp, and rises through the perforated
floor.   A primary brooder made on this plan is represented at Figs. 11, 12 and 13 ; Fig. 11 being a
side view of it ; Fig. 12 being a central longitudinal
section of it ; and Fig. 13 being a top view with the
brood-cover removed.   The brood-chamber A of
this brooder is enclosed between the brood-cover E
and the floor G ; about half of the floor being of
wire cloth or perforated tin supported upon a movable frame *a*.   Beneath the perforated floor is a hot-
air chamber C, which is supplied with air from a
lamp case D, beneath.   The hot gases from the lamp
chimney pass through a flue *b* in the hot-air chamber, and escape at the sides of the brooder.   The
flue is partially covered by a curved piece of tin
plate *m*, to protect the lamp chamber beneath from
dirt, and to distribute the hot air more equably.
The lamp has a kerosene burner of the smallest
size, and the wick must be kept down low, as very
little heat is sufficient to raise the temperature under
the brood-cover to 90° F., which is as hot as it
should be when the chickens are beneath it ; while
if the temperature be kept too high, the chickens

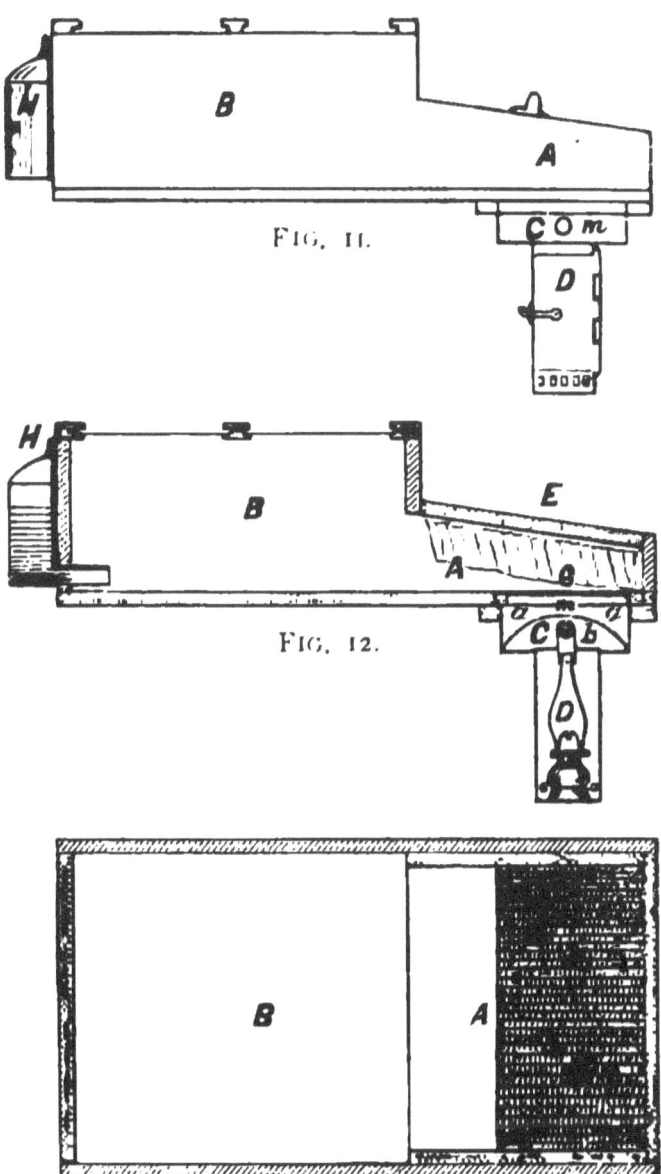

FIG. 11.

FIG. 12.

FIG. 13.

will sicken. The under side of the brood-cover should be lined with some soft material ; and those which the author has found best are two-ply ingrain carpet and blanket, either of which should be arranged in flutes, and secured to the brood-cover by rows of carpet tacks. The brood-chamber A is connected at its highest side with a small enclosed run B, open at the top, but provided with grooved slides for glass. The run should be partially covered with glass in cold weather, and in warm weather with a piece of wire net. During cold nights a cloth may be partially drawn over the brooder, but a portion of the top of the run must always be left open for ventilation. The opening between the brood-chamber and the run may have a piece of worsted fringe tacked along it ; this preserves the warmth in the brood-chamber, while permitting the passage of sufficient air for ventilation ; and it is surprising how quickly the chickens learn to run through the fringe.

Chickens immediately after being hatched are thoroughly exhausted by the efforts required to disengage themselves from the egg shells. They therefore require heat and rest, which are given by permitting them to remain in the trays of the incubator until their feathers become dry, or certainly for six hours. They do not require any food, and will rarely take any, until the day after their birth. They may then be placed in the primary brooder and food given to them, water being supplied by a font **H** at the end of the run. Sometimes one chicken will eat immediately ; if this be the case, all difficulty is over, because the pecking of food by one will teach the others to feed. If no one of the first lot pecks the food, they must be taught to do so by crumbling the food before them and tapping the floor with the end of the finger nail. When one is taught, it acts as a schoolmaster for all the others ; and when chickens are hatched successively, a few of each old brood should successively be left in the primary brooder to teach the newly-hatched chicks both to feed and to run into the brood-chamber for warmth. The use of the brood-chamber has to be taught the first chickens by putting them under the brood-cover by hand ; but they speedily find how comfortable it is, and the first chickens teach all the others, on the principle of the well known game of '' follow your leader.''

When the chickens become four or five weeks old, they should be removed to a secondary brooder, and subsequently to a third. The last two may be arranged on a level with the floor of a small house, which forms enclosed runs ; a pit being made beneath the brood-chambers for the lamp case. One kerosene lamp with a burner of small size is sufficient to heat two such brooders each four feet broad. If, however, the establishment be large enough to make it advisable to use a hot water or steam heating apparatus, a hot-water pipe or a steam pipe may be passed through the air-chamber under the brooder ; a few small holes being made in the bottom of the chamber under the pipe to admit fresh air. In such cases the lamp and its enclosure are superseded, and there is then no necessity for making the pit deeper than is sufficient to hold the hot-air chamber.

The chicken house or nursery, used by the author for raising about 250 chickens annually, is represented in cross section at Fig. 14 and in plan at Fig. 15 ; and it is large enough for 400 chickens, provided they be hatched in successive broods.   It has a roof sloping to the south, and formed in two pitches h, i.   The first pitch h is quite steep, and is formed alternately of hot-bed sashes six feet by three feet, and of solid panels six feet by three feet, made of boards battened at the seams.   The second pitch i is nearly flat, and is formed alternately of scuttle doors and fixed board panels, each three feet wide. The scuttle doors are hung on hinges at one edge, so as to open upward, and they are fitted with greenhouse lifting irons (Fig. 16), so that the sashes may be

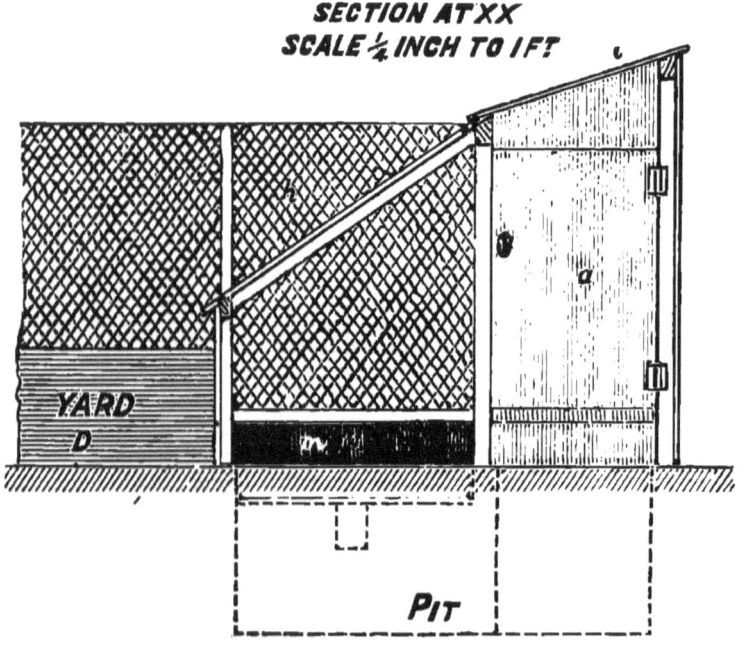

SECTION AT XX
SCALE ¼ INCH TO 1 FT

YARD
D

PIT

FIG. 14.—CROSS SECTION OF NURSERY.

raised and held open for ventilation. The low side
of this nursery does not exceed two and a half feet in
height ; while the longitudinal plate on which the
upper ends of the sashes are supported is only six
feet high ; and the highest side wall is seven feet.
These heights make the space under the roof high
enough for any practical purpose, because the portion under the second pitch is high enough to permit
an attendant to walk upright, and it is necessary to

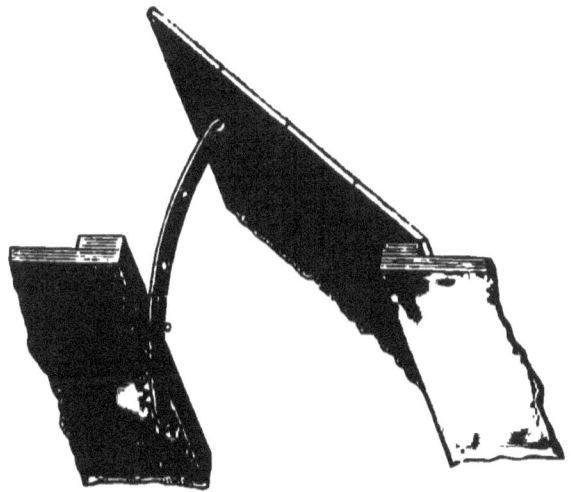

FIG. 16.—SCUTTLE DOOR.

pass beneath the lower pitch of the roof only when
the house is cleansed or the brood-covers are removed ; and then one naturally stoops to do the required
work, so that a greater height is unnecessary. This
nursery is divided into three sections A, B, C' (Fig.
15) of unequal sizes, the division being made by wire
net partitions fitted with plain battened doors a, b.
The rebates for the doors are made by nailing strips
upon the posts. Each door is fitted with a cord,

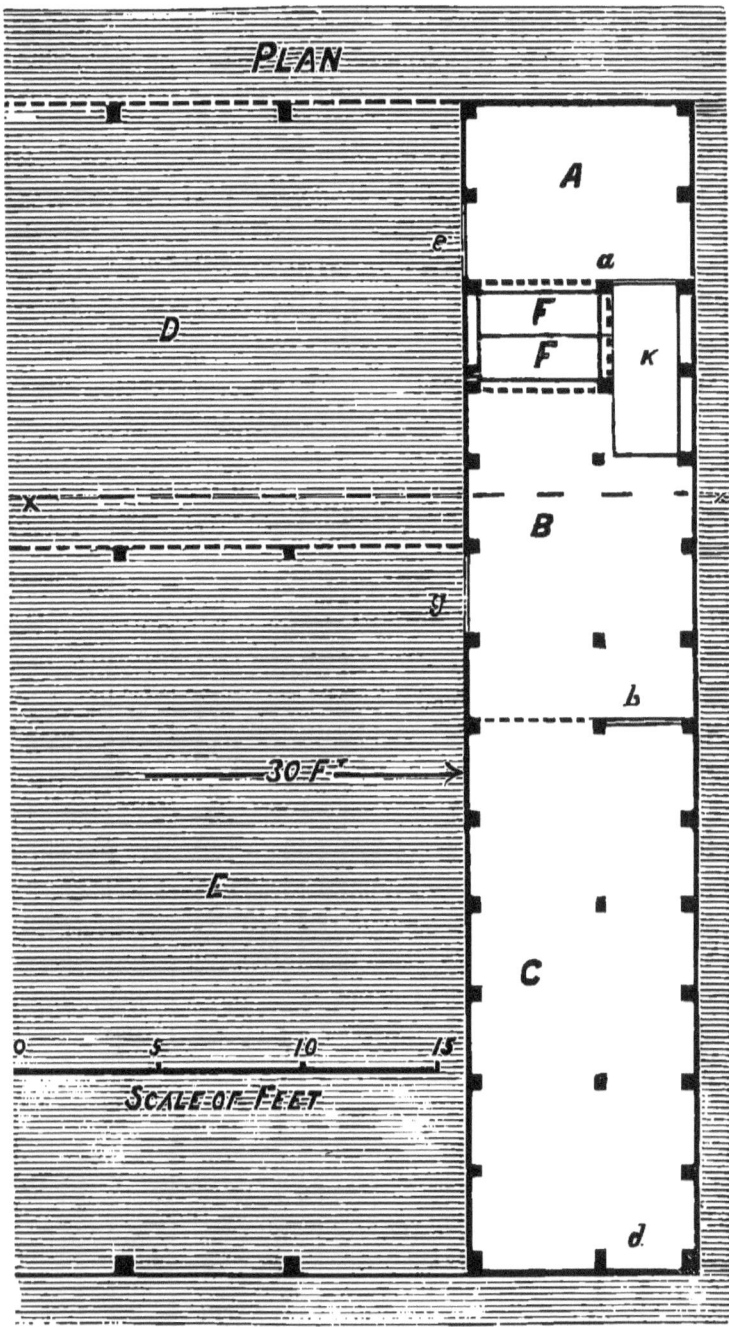

FIG. 15.

weight, and pulleys, so that it is self-closing. The
wire net and the doors do not extend down to the
floor, but terminate at cross bars *m*, about ten
inches from the floor. Removable board shutters
are applied to the spaces under these cross bars.
The smallest section A is the secondary section, for
chickens discharged from the primary brooder.
The central section B is appropriated to the largest
sized chickens that require a brooder ; and the largest
section C is used for chickens large enough to perch,
and is fitted with movable perches set fifteen inches
above the floor. The brood-chambers F, F of the
secondary and central sections are arranged back to
back over a pit represented in dotted lines in the
section. This pit is lined with rough hemlock
boards nailed to studs, and it is entered by steps
covered with a flat door K. The pit contains the
hot-air chamber, and the lamp case beneath it, and
access is had to the lamp by a door in the side of
the lamp case. The double brooder is represented
on a larger scale, and in section at Fig. 17. The hot-
air chamber for this brooder is represented in plan
at Fig. 18. The gases from the lamp chimney pass
through a pipe *m* which is bent in the form of a
square ring, and the gases escape through a vent
tube *n*. The hot-air chamber is covered with two
frames *a a*, Fig. 17, on which perforated metal is
tacked to form the perforated floors for the brood-
chambers ; and the front of each brood-chamber may
be enclosed by worsted fringe *l l*.

The under side of each brood-cover is lined with
ingrain carpet tacked in flutes so as to form a series
of inverted U-formed cells or channels, A A'. The

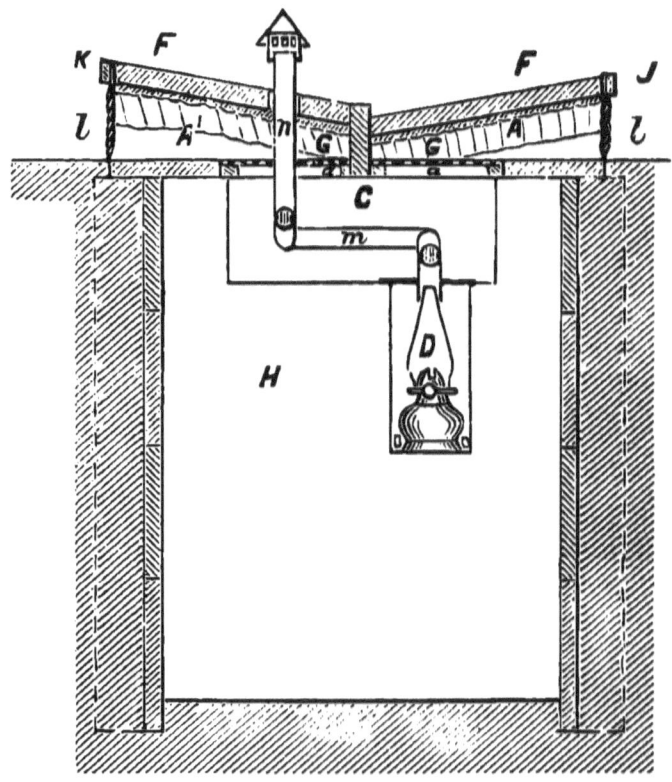

FIG. 17.

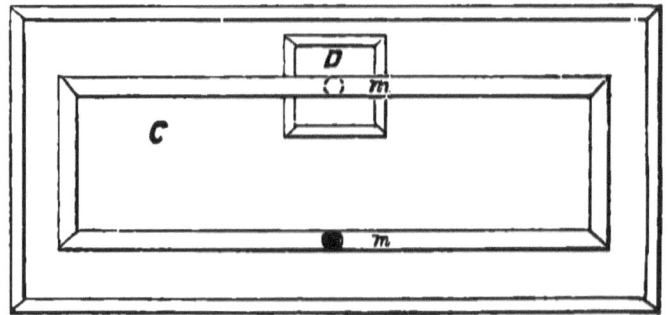

FIG. 18.—BROODERS.

floor of the nursery is formed of earth raised about
an inch above the natural surface, well rammed and
plastered about an inch thick with cement mortar ;
the earth having been permitted to dry thoroughly
before being plastered. The floor is covered with
coal ashes, some of which is greedily eaten by the
young chickens, and the same material is sprinkled
over the floor of the primary brooder. This last is
supported about breast-high upon a pair of rails
nailed to the posts of the secondary section A, so
that the establishment constitutes a complete nursery
for chickens from the earliest age to adolescence.

The secondary and central sections of the nursery
communicate with yards (D and E) by means of flap
doors (*e* and *g*), so that the chickens can be allowed
to run out in fair weather. The fences of the yards
are made of hemlock boards for two feet in height,
the edges of the bottom boards being sunk a little
in the earth so as to prevent the escape of chickens ;
while the rest of the fence is made of small meshed
wire net.

As the chickens grow, they are transferred from
the primary brooder to the secondary section A ;
thence to the central section B ; and from it to the
finishing section C, which communicates by a hole
under the front door *d*, with a large grass run of
two acres. About once a day a few spadefuls of
the soil of each yard are dug up to furnish fresh earth
for the young chicks to scratch in.

The whole nursery is made of common ten-inch
boards, machine planed, and nailed to posts planted
in the ground. The lower ends of the posts up to
six inches above the ground were given two coats of

coal tar dissolved in crude petroleum, and applied
with a brush while hot. This preparation strikes
into the wood rapidly, dries at the surface, and
renders the wood proof against rot for many years.
The seams between the boards of the roof are battened and the walls are lined with tarred felt. The
space over the large double brooder is enclosed with
removable frames covered with wire net to keep the
chickens from the top of the brood-covers. Each
brood-cover is fitted with a common iron trunk
handle, so that it can be readily lifted and removed
to enable the perforated floor to be cleansed.

This nursery was made long and narrow because
it was convenient to build it along a division fence,
the posts of which were incorporated in the back
wall of the building. If space could be conveniently
obtained, it would be better to make the building
of double the width and about half the length ; say
21 feet long by 16 feet broad ; and to give the roof
a double pitch in opposite directions from the
central line. The ground plan and perspective view
of a nursery of this description are given at Figs. 19
and 20. The two brood sections A, B, occupy half
of the building at one side of a central longitudinal
partition, and the finishing section C occupies the
other half. The doors *a*, *b*, of the first two sections
open into the finishing section C, which forms the
passage to them. The door *k* to the pit of the
double brooder is an upright door in the main partition. The yard D for the secondary section may be
at one side of the building ; and the yard E, for the
other brood section, may be at the rear end. The
front door may be at *d*. If wire net cannot be ob-

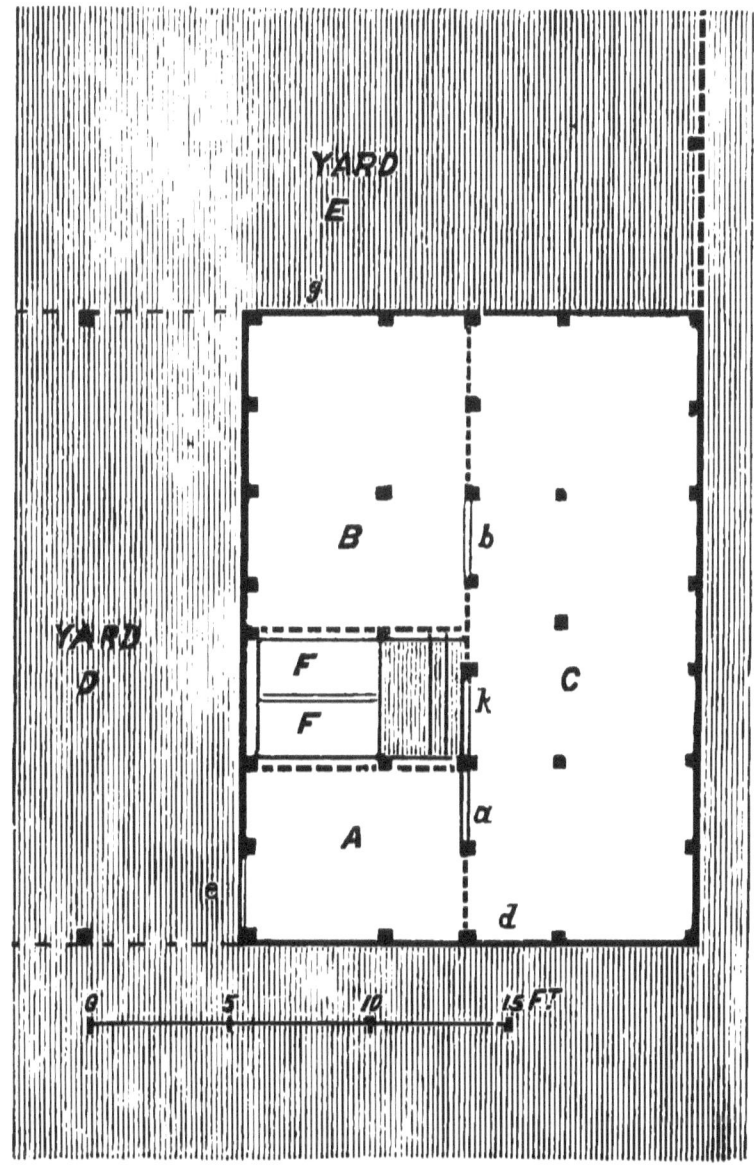

FIG. 19.—PLAN OF NURSERY.

tained for the partitions, or is deemed too costly, seine net, such as is used by fishermen and is made by machinery at a low cost, may be employed. Or, laths three quarters of an inch broad by half an inch thick may be employed. These can be procured from any manufacturing builder who has a small circular sawmill ; and if they are not dressed smooth at the edges, partitions made of them cost considerably less than when made of wire net.

The materials required for the double pitch nursery are as follows :

8 posts, each 9 feet 6 inches long.

10 posts, each 8 feet 6 inches long.

16 posts, each 5 feet long.

10 joists, 2 × 4 × 13 feet for plates on posts.

8 joists, 2 × 4 × 13 feet for rafters of first pitch.

3 joists, 2 × 4 × 13 feet for partitions.

66 pieces of novelty siding, 5 inches wide by 13 feet long.

38 boards, 10 inches wide by 13 feet long (faced on one side) for the roof and the scuttle doors.

7 boards for internal doors.

7 hemlock boards 16 feet long for pit.

450 running feet of batten moulding for roof.

150 square feet of net, or 75 laths $\frac{3}{4}$ × $\frac{1}{2}$ × 13 feet.

12 pairs of butt hinges, 3 × 3.

2 barrels of cement for floor.

The posts may be made of 2 × 4 joists, in which case there will be required 18 of 2 × 4 × 15 feet long for that purpose.

Instead of having a single yard for each of the first two sections of the nursery, it is better to have two yards for the secondary section A, and two for the

FIG. 20.—PERSPECTIVE VIEW OF NURSERY.

central section B.   The chickens can then be allowed access to each yard in alternate succession, say
two weeks to each.   This plan is advantageous,
because it obviates the danger of the yards becom-
ing foul from excessive use.   It is also advantageous
to have a few bushes in the yards for shade in hot
weather, one of the best plants for this purpose
being the common sumach.

The yard for the secondary section should contain
not less than 600 square feet of surface ; being, say
21 feet wide by 28 to 30 feet long ; or two yards
each of half this size may be used.   The yard for
the central section should be double the size of that
for the secondary section.   If the yards are too small,
they become foul before the close of the hatching
season, and the later chickens droop.   If this should
occur, either fresh ground must be provided, or the
ground of the yards must be spaded over immediately, so as to bury all foul matter and thus disinfect
the yards.   In such case, however, the chickens
must be supplied twice a day with fresh green food,
and all that is not consumed must be either dug
under or removed.   As soon as the youngest
chickens can be turned out of the yards, it is a good
plan to spade over the whole ground, and to sow it
at once with grass seed.   The first rains cause this
to sprout, and thus a fine plot of fresh grass is provided for the next year.

With a low-priced classifying nursery, such as
either of those above described, there is no difficulty
in raising chickens, if proper food be given them and
the place be kept clean.   If they are hatched too
early for grass, lettuce should be raised under cold

frames to supply them with green food ; because, although they will get along very well for three or four weeks without green food, yet as they grow it becomes a necessity ; and if it be not provided, they get a species of cholera infantum and die off. If proper food be supplied and ordinary care be taken, much fewer casualties occur than with chickens brought up by hens, and the labor of taking care of the same number is much less. Young chickens must have some animal food, and nothing is better for the purpose than the unfertile eggs taken from the incubator. These should be boiled hard at once, so that they will keep until wanted, when they should be chopped fine and mixed with Indian meal or oat grits slightly moistened so as to be crumbly.

A common coffee-mill should be screwed fast to one of the posts of the nursery for the purpose of cracking refuse wheat, so that a pan of coarsely cracked wheat may be continually kept within reach of the first two classes of young chickens. The quantity they will consume of it, even when other food is furnished in abundance, is surprising, and it appears to have a favorable effect upon their digestive organs. The chickens after leaving the primary brooder may be fed with what is commonly called " feed " mixed stiff with a little water, and containing a little bone meal ; or with a mixture of equal parts of corn meal and wheat bran, mixed in the same manner, care being taken to feed no more at any one time than they will eat up clean before the next feed is given. They should also have free access (as they grow larger) to cracked or whole light wheat in a feed hopper, or to a mixture of wheat and cracked corn. Occasionally a small quantity of animal food finely chopped should be given them, and a supply of clean water must be provided.

To raise chickens artificially with success there is one condition that is indispensable, and that is cleanliness ; for however much care be taken to supply proper food and warmth, young chickens will sicken and die unless their quarters be well ventilated and be kept clean. The ventilating brooder invented by the author supplies fresh warm air continually to the chickens under the brood-cover. The perforated floors of the brood-chambers should be brushed off daily with a whisk, and it is expedient to remove the brood-covers every morning for this purpose, and also because it is possible that a chicken may be trodden to death during the night ; although such a casualty rarely happens unless the chicken be sick. The daily cleansing of the brood-chambers is important, as it is bad enough for chickens to remain all night in the effluvia of their fresh droppings ; and the sanitary conditions may be imagined when the droppings are permitted to accumulate for several days in the moist warm air under a brood-cover. Occasionally the linings of the brooders should be sprinkled with carbolic soapsuds or with a weak solution of carbolic acid in water, and the perforated floor should be taken up and scraped, and then washed with the same material. After such sprinkling, the brood-cover should be exposed to the sun or be well aired, so that it may be dry before it is put in place. While the drying is being effected, the chickens should be kept from the brood-chamber by a piece of board. The floors of the run of the

primary brooder and of the nursery should be covered with either fine coal ashes, or dry earth, the
former being preferable, and fresh material being
occasionally added ; ashes which have been sifted
through a stone mason's sand screen, or a wire cloth
sieve of a quarter of an inch mesh, are quite fine
enough, as the small fragments are an advantage,
they being cracked and eaten by the young chickens.
The floors of the primary brooder and of the nursery should be raked over frequently with a fine-
toothed rake, and the droppings and foul ashes removed.   A good instrument for such raking may be
made by driving a row of two-inch wire nails half an
inch apart and half an inch deep into a strip of
wood, clipping off the heads of the nails evenly with
a cutting pliers, and fitting a small handle to the
rake head so made.   If lettuce or other cut green
food be used, the wilted stalks and remnants should
be regularly removed, as they tend to produce sickness.   All stale mixed food should be removed for
the same reason before fresh food is supplied.   If a
chicken be sick, it should be removed from the others
at once and kept in warm quarters until well.   With
ordinary care, cleanliness, and a supply of proper
food, sickness will rarely occur ; but it is a good
plan to have a spare primary brooder on hand, so
that if a chicken does sicken, it may be transferred
to it and kept warm until well.

A good chicken nursery is essential to the raising
of chickens artificially ; and unless one be provided,
it is practically useless to make the attempt, however costly an incubator be procured.

THE HATCHING SEASON.

THE thermostatic incubator furnishes the means of hatching chickens throughout the year, but there are certain peculiarities of the seasons in our Northern and Midlde States which do not render this course generally expedient. In order that young chickens may thrive, they must have warmth, plenty of exercise in the air, and green food. Plenty of exercise necessarily implies a large run, and such a run can be obtained in cold weather only by covering a large surface with glass. Persons who have cold graperies may use them with great advantage as runs for early chickens ; but those who do not possess such luxuries, and cannot afford the cost of a suitable building for an enclosed run of several hundred square feet, must content themselves with hatching chickens at seasons when those which are a month old can run out of doors without risk. On the other hand, the excessive heat of July and August is not favorable to the bringing up of very young chickens, and besides, the season is then so far advanced that unless the chickens are wanted for late broilers, they are not sufficiently advanced by the time winter sets in. Under these circumstances it is generally inexpedient in the Eastern, Northern, Middle, and Western States to start the incubator before the 1st of February, or to continue its use much after the 1st of

July. If started in February the season is generally sufficiently advanced to permit the chickens to run out in enclosed yards for several hours daily by the time they are old enough to be transferred from the primary brooder to the floor of the nursery. The enclosure of the yards with boards for a height of two feet, makes a shelter against cold winds, so that the chickens do not suffer as they would do without this protection ; but, even with this advantage, the chickens at first should not be allowed to run out except in fine weather, and should be called in long before sunset. If young chickens be called or whistled to whenever they are fed, they speedily learn what the sound means, and can be called in at any time by the same sound. They should be called and fed on damp food at least three times a day, and should have green food and crushed grain to peck at between feeds. With such treatment and cleanliness they will grow rapidly and will outstrip in size and vigor chickens raised by hens with the ordinary treatment.

There is another consideration which renders it inexpedient to commence the incubation of eggs in this latitude too early in the season. The eggs which are laid in the winter are laid almost exclusively by pullets of the preceding spring, and these are frequently unfertile. Thus, in February the author has frequently found three quarters of the eggs laid by pullets to be unfertile. As the season progresses, the proportion of fertile eggs increases, until in April nine tenths of the eggs will be fertile. Sometimes, however, cocks and hens show strange vagaries in mating, particularly when a single cock

is kept with several hens, the cock mating with
some one or more hens, and refusing to mate with
others, unless the favored hens be removed temporarily. Thus, in one instance noticed by the author,
a cock was placed with seven pullets. The eggs of
only two of these proved to be fertile. These two
were removed, whereupon the cock mated with the
remaining five, and their eggs all became fertile. In
another case, three Houdan pullets hatched from a
sitting of eggs procured from a noted breeder were
placed in December with a Houdan cock one year
older than the pullets, and four Brahma hens were
also given him. In due season the pullets began to
lay, but not one of the eggs proved to be fertile.
After several weeks the Brahma hens were taken
away. It was then noticed that the eggs of but one
of the pullets became fertile, and she had to be
taken away temporarily before the cock would mate
with the other two. This caprice or vagary in mating probably explains the fact that eggs purchased
in the spring of the year from the most respectable
breeders are frequently unfertile, particularly if the
females of the breeding pen consist partially or
wholly of pullets. Thus, on one occasion the author
purchased a sitting of eggs from a noted breeder,
and only four of the eggs proved to be fertile, the residue remaining clear, although placed in the incubator side by side with the others. In another case
eight fresh ducks' eggs given to the author by a
friend proved wholly unfertile, while the eggs of
ducks kept by the author and put into the incubator
at the same date and side by side with the others all
proved fertile. The above facts are important as

showing that the failure to hatch eggs is not necessarily the fault of the incubator, but is frequently due to other causes. In fact, when the eggs are put under hens, it is a very common circumstance to hear complaints to the effect that the eggs hatch badly, or that the owners have bad luck, particularly when the hens are set early in the spring.

If the breeding stock is kept in flocks containing several cocks, the absence of fertility is not so apt to occur, because the weaker cocks will mate with hens or pullets that are not appropriated by the stronger cocks.

APPENDIX.

Claims of United States patents granted to E. S. Renwick.

Patent No. 193,616, dated July 31st, 1877.

Improvements in incubators.

1. The combination, substantially as before set forth, of the incubating-chamber, the egg-holders, the heat-flue, and the waste-heat chimney.

2. The combination, substantially as before set forth, of the incubating-chamber, the egg-holder, the heat-flue, the waste-heat chimney, and the chimney-valve.

3. The combination, substantially as before set forth, of the incubating-chamber, the egg-holder, and the air-pipe arranged to supply air into the upper part of the incubating-chamber.

4 The combination, substantially as before set forth, of the incubating-chamber, the holder, and the ventilating-chimney arranged to discharge the air from the lower part of the incubating-chamber.

5. The combination, substantially as before set forth, of the incubating-chamber, the egg-holder, the ventilating-chimney arranged to discharge air from the lower part of said chamber, and the ventilating-valve which regulates such discharge.

6. The combination, substantially as before set forth, of the incubating-chamber, the egg-holder, the ventilating-chimney arranged to discharge air from the lower part of said chamber, and the air-supply pipe arranged to supply air to the upper part of said chamber.

7. The combination, substantially as before set forth, of the incubating-chamber, the egg-holder, and the water-tray ar ranged in the upper part of said incubating-chamber, whereby moisture is supplied above the level of the egg-holder.

8. The combination, substantially as before set forth, of the incubating-chamber, the egg-holder, the water-tray arranged in the upper part of the incubating-chamber, and the under water-tray.

9. The combination, substantially as before set forth, of the incubating-chamber, the egg-holder, the ventilating-chimney, and the thermostatic chamber, whereby the air escaping from the incubating-chamber is caused to pass through the thermostatic chamber.

10. The combination, substantially as before set forth, of the incubating-chamber, two egg-holders, the thermostatic chamber arranged between the said two egg-holders, and the ventilating-chimney communicating with said thermostatic chamber.

11. The combination, substantially as before set forth, of the incubating-chamber, the egg-holder, and two independent heaters having their ends which receive heat arranged at the opposite ends of the incubating-chamber

12. The combination, substantially as before set forth, of the incubating-chamber, the egg-holder, the water-tray, and the drain-pipe, whereby surplus water is conducted from the incubating-chamber.

Patent No. 210,559, dated December 3d, 1878.
Regulating mechanism for incubators, etc.

1. The combination, substantially as before set forth, of two thermostatic bars by means of a connecting lever, which has its fulcrum carried by one of said bars and its arm connected with the other of said bars.

2. The combination, substantially as before set forth, of a thermostatic bar arranged horizontally, with a counterpoise-weight.

3. The combination, substantially as before set forth, of

the engine-shaft, detent-motor, and engine-detent, whereby the detent-motor is wound up by the engine.

4. The combination, substantially as before set forth, of the engine, engine-detent, detent-motor, and regulator-detent.

5. The combination, substantially as before set forth, of the engine, liquid speed-controller, and engine-detent.

6. The combination, substantially as before set forth, of a thermostatic bar, regulator-detent, detent-motor, engine-detent, and engine.

7. The combination, substantially as before set forth, of the engine, liquid speed-controller, engine-detent, detent-motor, and regulator-detent.

8. The combination, substantially as before set forth, of the regulator-detent, detent-motor, engine-detent, engine, and valve.

9. The combination, substantially as before set forth, of a thermostatic bar, regulator-detent, detent-motor, engine-detent, engine, and valve.

10. The combination, substantially as before set forth, of the detent and the shifting weight.

11. The combination, substantially as before set forth, of the thermostat and the shifting weight.

Patent No. 215,070, dated May 6th, 1879. Improvements in chicken brooders.

1. The combination, substantially as before set forth, of the brooding-chamber, the brood-cover, and the perforated floor for the brooding-chamber.

2. The combination, substantially as before set forth, of the brooding-chamber, the brood-cover, the perforated floor for the brooding-chamber, and the hot-air chamber beneath the said floor.

3. The combination, substantially as before set forth, of the brooding-chamber, the brood-cover, the perforated floor of the brooding-chamber, and the run communicating with the said brood-chamber.

4. The combination, substantially as before set forth, of

the brooding-chamber, the brood-cover, the perforated floor of the brooding-chamber, the hot-air chamber, and the furnace.

Patent No. 217,148, dated July 1st, 1879.
Improvements in incubators.

1. The combination, substantially as before set forth, of the incubating-chamber, the egg-holder, the air-supply pipe, and the heat-flue arranged within the air-supply pipe.

2. The combination, substantially as before set forth, of the incubating-chamber, the egg-holder, and the heat-flue constructed to ascend to the upper part of the incubating-chamber and to spread therein laterally in the vicinity of the exit-tube, whereby the heat is more thoroughly distributed.

3. The combination, substantially as before set forth, of the incubating-chamber, the egg-holder, the heat-flue ascending in the incubating-chamber, and the water-tray applied to said heat-flue.

4. The combination, substantially as before set forth, of the incubating-chamber, the egg-holder, the heat-flue, the water-tray applied to said heat-flue, and the waste-heat chimney passed through said water-tray.

5. The combination, substantially as before set forth, of the incubating chamber, the egg-holder, the water-tray within the incubating chamber, the basin at the exterior of the chamber, and the water-fount.

Patent No. 224,224, dated February 3d, 1880.
Improvements in incubators. ·

1. The combination, substantially as before set forth, of the egg-holder of an incubator with supporting-rollers connected with the egg-holder by pivots, and with each other by connecting devices which cause them to revolve in the same direction.

2. The combination, substantially as before set forth, of the egg-holder of the incubator, the egg-supporting rollers, and

the elastic bands which connect said rollers together and cause them to revolve in the same direction with equal surface speed.

Patent No. 281,397, dated July 17th, 1883.
Improvements in thermostats for incubators.

· 1. The combination, substantially as before set forth, of the straight expansile strip of the thermostat, the lever and weight arranged to act upon one end thereof, and the adjusting lever and screw at the opposite end thereof.

2. The combination, substantially as before set forth, of the expansile strip of the thermostat and the frame thereof with a weight by which the said strip is subjected to a strong tensile strain.

3. The combination, substantially as before set forth, of the thermostat, the detent moved thereby, the revolving shaft carrying the detent-arms, the paddle-arms also carried by said shaft, the trough through which said paddle-arms move, and the engine-frame holding the said detent-shaft, detent-arms, paddle-arms, and trough, in their proper relative positions.

4. The combination, substantially as before set forth, of the walls of the incubator, the expansile strip of the thermostat enclosed therein, the weight operating upon one end of said strip to subject it to a tensile strain, and the adjusting screw which operates upon the other end of said strip and extends through the adjacent wall of the incubator.

Patent No. 281,398, dated July 17th, 1883.
Improvements in incubators.

1. The combination, substantially as before set forth, of the incubating-chamber, with two lamps, both arranged at the same end of said chamber and separated laterally for the purpose described.

2. The combination, substantially as before set forth, of the incubating-chamber, the heat-flue, the ventilating-chim-

ney, and the vent-pipe for the heat-flue arranged to deliver into the ventilating-chimney.

3. The combination, substantially as before set forth, of the egg-holder, the series of rollers thereof, and the turning device arranged within the walls of the egg-holder which enclose said rollers.

4. The combination, substantially as before set forth, of the incubating-chamber, the egg-holder thereof, the heat-flue arranged in the upper part of the incubating-chamber above the egg-holder, and the heat distributor arranged below the heat-flue between it and the egg-holder.

5. The combination, substantially as before set forth, of the egg-holders arranged back to back with a space between them, and the thermostat arranged between said egg-holders.

PRICE-LIST OF INCUBATORS, Etc.

Incubator complete; capacity,
 160 Eggs, - - - - $75.00

Registering Thermometer, extra, 8.00

Primary Brooder, complete, 2x4
 feet, - - - - - - 15.00

Secondary Brooder, with two
 brood chambers, 4 feet broad,
 ready for floor of Nursery, - 15.00

TERMS.—Cash (without discount) on de-
 livery in New York.

THE THERMOSTATIC INCUBATOR,

A Hand-book of Artificial Incubation.
> Paper covers, 36 cts. ; cloth, 56 cts.

By mail on receipt of post-office order or postal stamps (2c. each).

E. S. RENWICK,
19 Park Place, New York, N. Y.

www.ingramcontent.com/pod-product-compliance
Lightning Source LLC
Chambersburg PA
CBHW032205010726
47493CB00008BA/2838